Katy Watson grew up in Reading. She has worked on such underground feminist publications as *Shocking Pink* and *Bad Attitude*. She now works in TV listings and lives in Brixton with her two cats. This is her first novel.

HIGH ON LIFE
KATY WATSON

First published by The Women's Press Ltd, 2002
A member of the Namara Group
34 Great Sutton Street, London EC1 V 0LQ
www.the-womens-press.com

British Library Cataloguing-in-Publication Data
A catalogue record for this book is available from the
British Library.

ISBN 0 7043 4751 2

Typeset by FiSH Books, London WC1
Printed and bound in Great Britain by CPD Wales (Ltd), Ebbw Vale

CHAPTER I

Even the bloody air was painful. The cold outside was like a bucket of water in her face. It stung her skin and ran straight through her coat and in seconds it was chilling her bones. She pushed her hands inside her sleeves and set off slowly up the road. She'd already started to shiver and this hurt her too. Everything reminded her of heroin.

Even this early the streets were filling up as people began their celebrations for the night. A group of men and women came towards her on the pavement, their laughter bouncing off the walls. For a moment she was caught among them, muddled and claustrophobic, then they were past and she could breathe again. Across the road two men shouted at a car. The driver beeped and waved. Though it was barely eight o'clock, people were already stumbling drunkenly, with cans and bottles in their hands and clanking bags at their sides. Esther was appalled. She hated New Year's Eve and she knew well enough why that was. It was because it scared her.

It should have been five minutes' walk to the bus stop but instead it was taking forever. She'd felt exhausted the moment she'd stepped out of the door. At every side people were staggering and yelling and careering around and here she was, inching along like a woman of ninety, wincing at every noise. In spite of the cold, the effort of walking had brought her out in a wash of sweat down her back and her heart was racing as if she'd been sprinting. For a moment she stopped and leant against the wall of Barclay's Bank, avoiding the eye of the beggar beside her, then she dragged herself the last fifty yards to the bus stop and sat down with relief on the plastic seat. Somehow she'd neither collapsed along the way nor changed her mind and gone off to buy drugs instead. The miracle of it amazed her.

Between her home and here she'd passed half a dozen phoneboxes and all of them had reminded her of drugs. Over the years she'd made anxious calls from every one, trying to hurry dealers along who were always late. She'd stood and waited on every street corner, the minutes crawling by, willing the dealer's car towards her. As she'd left her flat tonight, the first passerby had looked like a junkie. Maybe they could score together: the thought had clicked in instantly. The teenage boy who passed her on a pushbike, surely he had to be a dealer? Even the streetlights reflecting on the wet tarmac had reminded her of a rainy night years ago, way back when it was all still new, when she'd scored on impulse at a friend's and run off home with it as a midweek surprise for Irfan.

It was a memory she hadn't even known she had. But a lot was coming back now, all at once and all unasked for.

Back in the flat she'd spent the whole day in terror, sure that today would be her downfall. How could she possibly stay clean amid this desperate festival of indulgence? Even cowering indoors she'd known she wasn't safe. She'd stepped around the phone as if it was a sleeping snake. Though she'd thrown away all her dealers' numbers when she'd started kicking, there was always some friend or acquaintance who could be called and persuaded to help her mess up. And her defences were like tissue paper. She was just trying not to stay still for long enough for the thought to take hold.

At the bus stop now the cold of the air against her eyeballs made her want to cry. A new year was almost here in New Brixton, where bars and clubs and restaurants rubbed sides these days with the beggars and the pound shops and the anger. The world was moving on. Would she be among those left behind?

Then the 37 came and that reminded her of heroin too. Many a time she'd made this trip to Peckham when she couldn't score in Brixton. The very ticket in her hand said she was on her way to senseless bliss. Everywhere she turned heroin was calling her name.

She was two weeks clean today.

And of course she shouldn't be visiting her junkie friend Darren, but it was bad enough already that she was planning to be sober; if she spent the evening alone it would surely destroy her. New Year's Eve is a dangerous time, when personal insights threaten like sea serpents, stirred up from the deep by the change from one year to the next. Which is why, like any sane person, she'd always protected herself with drink and drugs. But now superstition had her cornered, because the start of the year is full of omens, too, and tonight she knew that if she didn't pass through the curtain of midnight heroin-free, then her chances would be wrecked for the whole year to come. It was a night of possibilities, and most of them were bad.

The cold, steamed up bus turned a corner, past the multi-coloured neon lights of an off licence, more like something on Brighton seafront than the backstreets of south London. It sparked a memory of a summer night a year or two before, when she'd set off to Darren's for a weekend of fun while his

3

flatmates were away. How many times had she sat where she was now with her stomach full of butterflies, half from anxiety, half anticipation, cursing the bus for going so slowly?

It was terrifying. Because every moment of her life these past few years had had the same purpose. For so long every problem had had the same solution. Now every impulse of her life would have to change: everything she did and everything she was. Surely the task was too big for her. How was she ever going to learn to be so different?

It was nothing that she hadn't thought ten thousand times already these last two weeks, but all the same her heart began to flutter. Sweat pricked at her armpits as she staggered once again before the immensity of what she had to do. And as her panic increased, so it frightened her all the more, because panic was her enemy and she'd forgotten how to fight it.

The only answer she remembered was sedation and she had nothing left to do it with. She'd started out her kicking with a phial of Spanish valium, a pleasant and useful drug, but that was long gone. She had no choice. Getting off the bus at the terminus, she headed for the nearest off licence and bought a half bottle of cheap whisky with a picture of a stag on the label. Then she headed down Peckham Road, past more noisy, drunken revellers, and into the unmapped, half-demolished maze of Peckham North Estate. By the time she reached the low block where Darren lived she was dizzy and light-headed. The tiredness was in her bones. It felt as though some element crucial to her body's make-up had been taken away and it was having to rebuild itself from scratch. Which, of course, was almost exactly what was happening.

Climbing the concrete stairs she had to rest at every landing. And again she was reminded of heroin, of that acrid tang that sometimes reaches your mouth before the hit hits your brain. Now she could taste it in anticipation, like Pavlov's dog. How was she ever going to get free of this? She was haunted and possessed.

Darren opened the door to her. He was clearly in the party mood. Along with his usual dirty army pants, he had on glittering red earrings, matching nail varnish and a shimmering turquoise blouse.

'Hiya, Esther, how ya doing?' He crushed her in a hug.

As he let her go she peered into his eyes. The pupils were pinpricks in the deep brown. She was both jealous and alarmed. The heroin was so close. There it was, in his blood, right beside her.

'Gotta drink,' she announced, holding up the whisky bottle to illustrate her intention.

Darren shrugged. 'OK.' He had the happy indifference to alcohol of someone on a better drug.

The kitchen reminded her of the two of them cooking up over the gas ring when no one else was in, ready to jump at the sound of a key in the door. Darren handed her a glass and she poured a large measure. Lovingly hand-crafted from a big vat of chemicals. She coughed a little as it attacked her throat.

In the flat's small living room Darren's so-called flatmates, Ross and Brenda, were sat in front of the television with beers in their hands. 'So-called' because in fact it was their flat and Darren was sleeping on the sofa while he waited to get housed. But he'd been there so long you could forget this.

'How are you, Esther?' asked Brenda, looking at her carefully. Darren's view, based on the rock-solid evidence that he liked to think so, was that his flatmates had no idea of his drug use. But it seemed he'd neglected to explain this to them.

'I'm fine,' she answered, aware that this was possibly unconvincing. Her face felt taut and bloodless and the whisky in her hand had clearly not been produced with fun in mind. But it was none of Ross and Brenda's business to be seeing her in this state. They were violating her right to fall apart with privacy and dignity. What was the world coming to when you couldn't even lose your grip in peace?

She sat down in a corner, upright and terrified on a wooden chair. Darren squeezed onto the sofa next to Brenda. Esther lit a cigarette, which shook in her hand. She sipped at the whisky as fast as she could stand to.

'What are you two up to tonight?' asked Brenda.

'Uh, I don't know.' Instinct said it must be something she shouldn't. Then she remembered what night it was. 'Oh. We're going to a party somewhere.' Though a fatal overdose or committal to a mental institution seemed just as likely. And possibly preferable.

Slowly her words made the journey to Darren's consciousness. 'Oh, yeah.' He considered the matter carefully. 'Well, I think Vin's coming round and he's taking us to some party in Camberwell. Or else we might be going to this one that Jaks knows about.'

Esther poured another glass of whisky. Maybe it was good that it was so toxic and nasty. It might stand more chance of burning out whatever it was that was wrong with her. And maybe if she got drunk she might at least get a night's sleep, which would be a first since she'd started kicking. On TV a sitcom was reaching its climax. A man had just run back into his kitchen to find his dinner in flames on the cooker. She started to feel a touch calmer. There was no reason why she shouldn't be able to get through the night now. She had a strategy. It occurred to her that she should ask what Ross and Brenda were doing tonight, but it just seemed so far from the point.

'We're going to Animal Farm,' said Brenda, undeterred.

'Cost enough,' muttered Ross.

'Well, what do you expect? It's New Year's.' She turned back to Esther. 'But we got a video out to watch first.' She seemed to stop short.

'Uh huh,' Esther nodded, desperately uninterested.

The credits were rolling for the sitcom. Ross and Brenda had gone quiet.

'It's *Trainspotting*,' said Brenda eventually, to her knees.

Ross shrank a little in his seat. 'Everything else was out. And I never saw it.'

A spoof gameshow was just starting up. The mischievous host was already sprinkling something that looked like wood shavings on the shoulders of one of his guests. Esther lit another cigarette. Darren was the only one who seemed unfazed. He looked just as relaxed as before.

Ross put the video in and fast-forwarded through the adverts. Esther had seen the film before, with Irfan. If there was any film a junkie would have seen in the last ten years, this was it. Just as Mafiosi watch *The Godfather*, so junkies watch *Trainspotting*. If they can get round to it, that is. And they put the posters up in their rooms. They are pleased that someone is thinking of them: it's nice to be catered to in your leisure time.

The opening sequence was just as Esther remembered. Ewan McGregor and his friends are running through the streets of Edinburgh, being chased by the police. Ewan is hit by a car, but he doesn't care. He just laughs in the face of the camera. Then Iggy Pop comes in singing 'Lust for Life', which sounds like adrenalin recorded, and it is clear that heroin addiction is the most exciting life in the world.

Then the scene changed and a group of people were sitting around in a dirty flat shooting up and talking about James Bond. As far as she could tell, she had never seen this scene before in her life. Was it possible she'd watched some different version of the film? One by one the actors took their shots and pretended to feel orgasmic or else fell over backwards on the floor. Esther smiled a little: we can't all be experts. But all the same, this imitation reminded her of what it was like when that hot joy exploded in your head. Was she really never going to do that again?

The doorbell rang and Brenda went to answer it. Darren's friend Vin stumbled into the room. In one hand he was carrying a bag bulging with bottles. In the other he held an open bottle with a paper bag wrapped around it.

He managed to focus first on Esther, but evidently wished he hadn't. He searched around the room for a friendly face.

'Hey, Darren, man. Like the earrings.' He slid down onto the floor next to the sofa and took another swig from his bottle.

The film continued through one scene and then another, but still Esther didn't recognise any of it. It was a little unnerving. Had she really been that stoned when she'd watched it? She turned to see what Darren was making of it and found that the room lagged behind now as she moved her head. At last. But of course it wasn't what she wanted: it wasn't smack. Smack numbs you and calms you and wraps you away in an embrace of perfect peace. But alcohol takes away the boundaries and hard edges of things, dissolves your control and leaves you swimming, liable to do anything. Once upon a time, Esther had been happy to drink. Before she ever took smack she used to drink a lot; she'd accepted that this was what she had to do to hold things together. But heroin had changed all that and now the whisky was making her uneasy. It was taking away her resistance to enchantment.

On the screen now Ewan was cooking up a shot. It was dark brown, pasty and opaque as it filled the syringe. Esther almost gagged. No one in their right mind would inject a shot like that. He had clearly been ripped off.

'Bloody hell,' exclaimed Darren in horror, then stopped

himself short, not wishing to give the game away to his flatmates.

The doorbell rang again. A man Esther didn't know bounced into the room.

'This is Andy,' Brenda introduced him.

'All right, mate, all right,' he nodded heartily around the room. His face was shining with sweat and his pupils were huge, dark holes. He was chewing gum vigorously. Esther couldn't imagine anything worse than what was going on in his head.

'Do you want yours now?' he asked Ross and Brenda as he sat down on the floor. 'They're pukka, you know, bloody pukka.'

Ross shook his head.

'Nah, not just yet,' said Brenda. 'We'll wait till we get there.'

They carried on watching the video. But now Esther was getting frightened. The magical romance that is heroin was infecting her more with every breath. She was breathing it in and in again; there was no way to stop it. The sight of a needle on the screen reminded her how wondrous it is to pierce your skin and send that tide of love hurrying through your veins. Pale, bare arms reminded her how her skin longed to be broken, how dull and flat things are when you're stuck on the surface. The scene of an overdose, though she felt a lift of superiority because it looked like no overdose she'd ever seen, reminded her what a beautiful dream destruction is, far more beautiful than life.

For the past two weeks she'd been trying to forget this. She'd been trying to hold tight to another knowledge: that addiction is monotony and fear, boredom and humiliation. The slow pursuit of death through a life both sordid and dull. But now the whisky was dissolving this reason away and her love was making her feverish. She remembered that heroin is the most fabulous madness this life has to offer, a madness so beautiful it is better than sanity. The whisky was just a mockery of this bliss and it was washing away her defences.

A shudder ran through her. She pushed herself to her feet and picked up the bottle of whisky. In the kitchen she poured it down the sink. She tried to steady her thoughts. Her head was spinning. She rubbed the inside of her forearm, full of longing. Maybe Darren had left something lying around. She cast her eyes around the kitchen, as if a needle or a wrap or just a little tiny pill might somehow appear. However was she going to stop this?

She tried to gather some composure and guided herself back into the living room. Inexplicably, the others were still watching the video as if they hadn't noticed anything.

'D'you wanna beer?' offered Ross. A few empty bottles were clustered by his chair.

Esther stared at him. It was amazing: he didn't seem to be joking. Her lip curled. 'No.'

Ross shrugged and turned back to the screen.

Seeing little option, Esther did the same. The film was reaching its end now and Ewan was doing a voiceover claiming that real life, with all its shoddy prizes, its wretched routines and sad materialism, was actually better than drug addiction. Esther was disgusted. This was just lame. The film had made some sense up till now, but this part didn't work at all. Maybe it was meant to be ironic, but she couldn't see it. Yet how could anyone possibly find this mocking list of life's supposed benefits more appealing than heroin?

The credits rolled.

'That was good,' said Darren.

'Cool,' said Andy, still chewing.

Bar the first two minutes, Esther had remembered not a single frame.

'God, is that the time?' said Brenda. 'I'd better go and get ready.'

Ross stopped the video and the TV came back on loudly. Something was happening with a studio audience. Brenda went off to the bedroom. The rest of them sat watching television, except for Vin, who seemed to be asleep. Esther wondered vaguely whether Darren was going to make some move to get them out to join the night's fun. Not that she actually wanted to go out, but on the other hand she didn't actually want to be anywhere.

Then in the same train of thought it occurred to her that Darren must have some needles hidden around the place. Maybe if she just pretended to shoot up it would give her some relief. This was the answer, of course: it was brilliant. It would be heaven on earth, it would soothe this madness away. To tie up, tap up a vein, find blood with the needle like a prospector striking oil. Darren's possessions were in a pile of sports bags and bin liners stuffed beside the sofa, where he slept. The easiest thing would be just to ask him, but she couldn't face it. If only this bunch of idiots would fuck off out of here, she would have a chance to look. What was the matter with them, sitting there like stuffed dummies?

In another flash of insight it came to her: he might not keep his needles in here. In fact, the bathroom was the obvious place, since that was where he usually shot up. Secretly, of course. She got up as slowly as she could, trying to act casual.

But in the bathroom there wasn't much scope for hiding anything. Though the bathroom cabinet was well stocked with such items as Malathion Liquid for treatment of scabies, half-used bottles of hair dye, ageing dental floss and so forth, it would have been an utterly useless place to hide drug paraphernalia. She stood on the bath to look on top of the cabinet, just in case, and checked behind the toilet and even in the cistern, but she knew in her heart it wasn't going to happen. Sitting on the side of the bath, she held her head in her hands. She was shaking all over. She needed this to work.

But this was ridiculous. What was she doing in the bathroom anyway? The kitchen would be a far better place for him to hide things. She could picture him taking his first shot of the day in there when he got up, around two, while Ross and Brenda were out at work. It made sense: it was like breakfast.

In the kitchen she felt dizzy with hope. It was full of hiding places. Being as quiet as she could, she started to look through the cupboards: behind stacks of bowls and plates, among mugs, tinned beans and spaghetti, spices, gravy, packets of rice and pasta. A box of cornflakes set her heart beating even faster: it was Darren's favourite food; they must be in there, underneath the packet. But no. She steadied herself on the worktop for a moment. Then she got down on her knees, quietly quietly, and started looking through the bottom set of cupboards. Pans and mixing bowls seemed a likely place: there was room in them to hide a packet of one mils. But one after another they came out empty. She put them on the floor so as to get right to the back of the cupboard. But still nothing.

The last possible place was the cupboard under the sink. It wasn't tidy in there. She took out old dusters, bottles of sink cleaner, bleach, methylated spirits, carpet shampoo, polishing spray with three-day dust guard, tins of varnish, gloss paint, Brillo pads, a disintegrating sponge, a bucket and an old washing-up bowl. But it was unbelievable: there was nothing in there. She sat down on the floor, with pots and pans and cleaning materials spread out around her, wracking her brains for where else she could search. Her head was spinning worse than before.

She heard footsteps in the hall. Before she could move, Darren appeared in the doorway.

'Bloody hell, Esther, what are you doing?'

'Nothing.' Who the hell was he to be looking at her like that? And what was he doing here anyway?

'Er, sorry,' he stuttered. 'I just thought...' He gestured lamely at the contents of the cupboards arranged on the floor.

Running on autopilot, Esther raised an eyebrow. She was still sat motionless on the floor.

'OK, well, I'll just let you, er...whatever.' He nodded and kept on nodding as he backed out of the room.

However had she got here?

Back in the living room she drew desperately on her cigarette. She had poured herself a glass of water in the hope that it would help her sober up. Brenda reappeared wearing tight trousers and sparkly grips in her hair. Ross and Andy got up to join her.

'Have a good night,' said Brenda as they left.

'Yeah, have a good one,' said Ross.

Darren was reclining on the sofa. 'Mm, thanks,' he murmured.

Vin moved his head slightly, without opening his eyes.

Esther tried to make her face smile, but sensed it might not have worked.

On TV now a man was pretending to be a middle-aged Latin singer. He was wearing fake tan, a dark wig, a satin shirt open to his stomach and a big gold medallion around his neck. The doorbell rang and neither Darren nor Vin moved. Reluctantly she went to answer it. Shouting and laughter echoed in the hall. She considered pretending there was no one in, but they pressed the doorbell again and held it down. Looking through the spy hole she recognised Tony and Paula, two friends of Darren's.

They fell in through the door with their arms around each other. Another friend swayed in after them.

'Hello, you're whassaname,' Paula informed her as they passed, bouncing from wall to wall down the hallway and into the living room. Tony and Paula landed on top of each other next to Darren on the sofa, and their friend slid to the floor. Esther headed for her seat in the corner, feeling more sober by the second.

'Hey, Daz,' yelled Paula, embracing him around the neck, 'Happy New Year! 'Sit midnight yet? We gotta get t'a party. Wake up, Vin!'

'Don't kick him!' said Tony from underneath her.

''M not kicking him, jus' waking him up with my foot. Watch out, you're spilling it! This is Magda.'

'D'you want some?' offered Magda, waving what appeared to be a bottle of Coke. Vin pulled himself slightly upright and accepted her offer. Darren and Esther both declined.

'Where we going, then, Daz?' asked Tony.

'Er, Vin knows. Vin!'

There was a pause.

'Uh, what?'

'Are we going to that one in Camberwell?'

Vin seemed to be receiving his words at the end of a transatlantic phoneline. There was another pause. 'Which one? Oh, shit. Rob was menna ring me.'

'We've gotta party!' shouted Magda.

'You're menna be taking us,' reprimanded Paula jovially, pushing Darren from side to side.

'Take us t'a party!' Magda reiterated. 'What time is it?'

'Anyone want some speed?' Tony started searching his pockets, as well as he could with Paula sitting on top of him. 'Fucking... where's it gone?'

'Party!'

'Ow, stop kicking me.' Vin made another effort to sit up straight. 'D'you want me to ring Jaks? Mmph.' He suddenly put his hand over his mouth, struggled to his feet and ran out of the room. Magda passed the bottle to Paula, who took a swig and passed it to Tony. On television Denise Van Outen was discussing her New Year's resolutions. Angus Deayton announced that it was twenty minutes to go. Esther's sobriety was coming on a treat.

'D'you think I should finish getting ready?' asked Darren.

Vin came back into the room, his hair wet and his face pale. He picked up the phone and started to dial.

'Urg, you're crushing me,' said Tony.

Now Carol Smillie was beaming at the camera. 'Welcome to a star-studded Hogmanay special, live from Edinburgh Castle.' She radiated wholesome cheer and, of course, Scottishness.

'Hallo!' beamed a man next to her in a kilt.

'Switched off,' announced Vin. 'I've left a message on whatd'youcallit.'

'I can't find that wrap,' said Tony. 'I think I've lost it.'

'Edinburgh is literally buzzing with hundreds of thousands of revellers,' said Carol Smillie.

'Stop hogging that bottle, Magda,' said Paula.

'I've got a kind of idea where it is,' said Vin. 'We could just walk around. We're bound to find something.'

'... Wild boys Duran Duran!' cried Carol. Inside the castle Duran Duran started to sing 'Rio'. A suit of armour stood next to them on the stage.

Esther felt all hope deserting her. She was ludicrously sober. Clearly this world was nothing but pointlessness.

'Sure you don't want some?' asked Magda, waving the bottle in her direction.

Esther smiled a freezing smile at her stupidity. Of course she didn't want any. She didn't like alcohol. She didn't like speed. And she didn't like bloody ecstasy. She liked heroin.

Carol Smillie introduced the velvety-voiced Sarah Brightman.

Sarah sang her song, backed by a male-voice choir. She had her arms stretched out sideways and was swaying from side to side, possibly pretending to fly, as a wind machine ruffled her hair.

'Oh shit,' said Magda and staggered out of the room. The sound of vomiting reached them from the hall.

Esther realised with utter certainty that she had been insane not to get stoned. She could think of nothing now but heroin.

'D'you think we should do something?' said Tony.

Heroin, wonderful heroin, thought Esther.

'Sorry,' said Magda, coming back into the room.

Darren pushed himself slowly out of his chair and left the room.

Esther saw her chance and rushed after him. In the dimness of the hall by the bathroom door she grabbed his arm.

'Darren, please, hang on a minute.' She could hardly breathe. 'Listen, have you got anything?'

'Have I . . .? Er, no. Sorry. I took it all earlier. You should've asked. It was nice gear, though.'

Her spirits sank to the ocean floor.

Back in the living room she took her upright place amid the chaos of prone bodies.

Carol Smillie's co-host had turned out to be a comedian. 'The thing about New Year's resolutions, Carol,' he was saying, 'is that they're like wind. If you break them, it's best to do it in private.'

'I think it's time for something a little more serious,' said Carol and introduced a gospel choir doing a song called 'To the Rock'. As they sang, the picture cut to a shot of the castle on top of its rock.

Esther decided to stay over and score with Darren the next day.

'And now,' said Carol, 'there's just enough time to reflect on the year that's past as the lone piper plays 'Amazing Grace'.'

Rising through the cold Scottish air, the song was suddenly slow and terribly moving. It was the last thing Esther was expecting. The room fell quiet. Esther couldn't stop herself. Tears streamed silently from her eyes and down her cheeks. She was crying for that year and for so many other years before it, for the time that was lost and wasted and for all that she had lost besides. She felt so tired, all worn out and used up by too much living and too much fooling around with death. Luckily no one seemed to notice the tears on her face.

The chimes of Big Ben came in over the end of the bagpipes. Paula, Tony and Magda all started shouting at once.

'Toast! We gotta have a toast!'

The room was a mess of arms and legs as they all searched around for glasses and tried to fill them.

Esther raised her glass of water and waited.

The last chime of the clock rang out and fireworks went off over Edinburgh Castle.

Looking forward to nothing but when Darren's dealer would turn on his phone the next day, Esther lifted her glass half an inch higher. The others were still busy untangling themselves and sharing out the right number of glasses, so she proposed the toast herself.

'Happy New Year,' she said, unspeakably weary.

The others clinked their glasses as best they could. 'Happy New Year,' they chorused. 'Yeah, happy New Year.'

CHAPTER 2

When she woke up two days later it was already dark. The clock beside her bed said ten to six. She rolled onto her back. Her face and chest where she had been lying were wet with sweat. The pale orange glow of street lights leaked through her curtains and the sound of traffic grumbled from the main road. Further away a police car turned on its siren. The weight of her mistake came down on her like the falling sky. She had messed up and now everything was different.

And here they were, herself and this fact, together in the same room with no distance to defend her. Even as she faced the matter of how, with this one act, she had so disastrously changed the shape and colour of the world, another regret rose in her mind. Yesterday, while stoned and confident, she had washed the remains of the heroin down the sink to protect herself from using it today. It was a foresight that had strangely failed to anticipate the hangover which was now trampling her under its hooves. Not to mention the general realness of the non-stoned condition, which benefits so greatly from medication. She must never take heroin again, that was true. But it would have been a whole lot better if never could have started tomorrow.

Presently she realised she was dehydrated, which wasn't surprising since most of her bodily fluid seemed to have seeped out through her skin while she was sleeping. As she got to her feet a headache gripped her skull. The inside of her mouth tasted of burning tyres. She felt groggy and unsteady and her body ached as if it had been violently attacked. As, of course, it had. Maybe there had been a quality problem, or maybe this was just the natural result of intravenous heroin use. To be honest she had never been sure. In the kitchen she drank a glass of water. A minute later she vomited it up, as clear and cold as when it had gone down.

Her reflection in the bathroom mirror was no better than it should have been. People had sometimes told her she was attractive, but she had never seen it. She found her Plain Jane features too severe, too thin-lipped, her straight brown hair too dull. Her eyes were a grey that was clear but not warm. She might have granted herself handsome at best. But now her face was as pale as a dead person's, with a sheen of oily sweat. Her pupils were huge and terrified, the opposite of the safe, contracted pinheads of heroin use, which so sensibly shut out as much of the world as possible. Now they were letting everything in, with no filtration, magnifying it. She washed her face and headed for the sofa.

Once again TV would have to be the embrace that nursed her through the evening. She settled first on a documentary about the wildlife of Madagascar. It showed creatures so beautiful they tugged at her heart. In lush jungles and glassy waterways there were round-eyed lemurs, velvety golden cats, iguanas, giant boas, bats, tortoises, glorious serpent eagles: a diversity like no other place on earth, the narrator said. Then, as the programme neared its close, he explained that multinational companies had been granted licences to move in by the impoverished government and much of this would soon be destroyed. Fat tears slid down Esther's face. How did people survive in this world with no protection? Would she ever be able to get used to it?

Next she was offered family movies too frightening for words and a home makeover show she'd seen before. She ended up with a docusoap about an emergency breakdown recovery service. It was certainly easier on the emotions. This was followed by a compilation of clips from shop security cameras, then a quiz show about TV, then things got slightly less exciting with a sitcom set in a tax office. At which point she went to bed.

But of course she couldn't sleep. One of the greatest joys of scoring yesterday had been the holy blessing of falling asleep the moment she had closed her eyes, the only time this had happened since she'd started kicking. Now, alone in the dark and starkly awake, her mind returned to her crime of the previous day. How was it possible that actions, once committed, were so unchangeable? She could hardly believe it. The fact was like a brick wall which sent her mind bouncing off it. How could it be true that she couldn't go back and undo what she had done? Coming round from a night's discomfort on Darren's floor, she wouldn't have woken him up and hassled him to get on the phone. She wouldn't have sat there, jaw set, angry and disgusted and determined to do the wrong thing. She'd just have picked herself up, trudged up to the bus stop and come home, tired and shaky but with her hope intact. She'd still have been in with a chance then, whereas now she wasn't so sure.

She turned from her side to her front to her other side and then back again, but she couldn't get comfortable. She turned the light back on and tried to read, but somehow *The Brothers*

Karamazov wasn't holding her attention. Strangely during her kicking she hadn't managed the serious reading that she'd hoped. As her mind wandered, her pulse began to accelerate. In the dark again, she stared up at the ceiling, wishing she had just a tiny dose of any kind of opiate to help her sleep. Just thirty milligrammes or so of codeine would have done the trick, or the smallest dab of heroin, just a few molecules really.

It's a peculiar cruelty that you can't sleep when you're coming off heroin. An exact and crucial piece of cruelty, because if it weren't for that the whole thing might be feasible. But night-time comes and goes with no relief. The torture simply continues, a violation of nature, so that after a couple of nights you feel utterly deranged. Your mind is as brittle as baked paper and time goes out of shape, stretching and contracting like an earthworm. Certain ideas seem strangely reasonable. You realise that the best way to stop taking drugs would actually be to take some now, just the once, to get over this bad bit...

Now, as Esther lay alone in her bed, the mattress still damp and foul from her kicking, she felt so tired that she thought she might die of it. If she'd still owned anything of value, which she didn't, she'd have exchanged it all for a sound night's sleep. She'd have sold her soul, except that no one seemed interested in buying it. Maybe the insomnia was going on too long. Was this normal? Maybe it should be better by now. Maybe she had taken too many drugs, for too long, and it had damaged her brain's chemistry for good, so that she'd never be able to sleep properly again. There was no reason, after all, why her body should be able to cope with such abuse with no lasting ill effect. In which case she'd have to take something to help her sleep for the rest of her life, and this something might as well be heroin. So the most sensible thing would be to catch a late bus up to Darren's place now. It was virtually a medical fact. This was how it would have to be and there was no point prolonging the agony. She'd tried to give up, but it just wasn't going to be possible.

And this was exhausting too: the business of remembering that the answer was always meant to be no. However convincing the arguments her mind put forward, her response was always meant to be the same. When was this war of trickery going to end? Or, more precisely, when would it no longer be the case that, just as a compass needle points north, so every atom of her mind and body was directed towards heroin? Maybe it should be getting better by now. Maybe it never would and she was just a hopeless case and she might as well get the bus up to Darren's place now...

It couldn't be denied, it took it out of you.

For the first few days of kicking she'd simply been too ill to leave the house. Every particle of her had been screaming for heroin, of course. There was nothing going on but that. No other thought or feeling stood a chance. But having destroyed all her dealers' phone numbers with a thoroughness borne of experience, meaning she'd torn them out in strips from her address book and burnt them, or at least scribbled them out five times over with biro, she'd only have been able to score by going out to see Darren or some other local junkie. Which, since she could barely make it to the toilet and back, was physically impossible. Which was exactly what she'd counted on.

But as the life force returned to her body by the tiniest degrees, so it seemed to transmute itself instantaneously into the will to go out and buy drugs. The nights were when it hit her hardest. By day, who knows why, she could restrain her psyche's demands with something slightly like sanity, but night-time to her craving was like the full moon to a werewolf.

It had built up steadily day by day until, on her tenth day clean, she began to think she was going to lose the fight. It was a couple of days after Christmas and Brixton was still quiet, as people spent the holiday outside London. All day she'd felt this madness rising higher inside her, cutting off her breath, threatening to flood out her reason. She was out of valium now and all she had instead was a little plastic bag of herbal tea from the drug project. She didn't feel that heroin addiction was suited to treatment with herbs. It seemed to call for chemicals, and powerful ones at that. This particular tea was meant to have a calming effect, but instead there was just this panic, rising and rising. The day was so damned long. And all the time, hour after hour, there was her heart racing, her breathing fast and short and useless and her mind whirling with the news that this wasn't going to work, she was too fucked up, this was something she'd never get out of.

By five o'clock a bargain was taking shape in her head. She'd make some more herb tea and if she didn't feel any better by six, then she'd be allowed to do something about it. No one could say she hadn't tried. But as six o'clock approached, she began to see what a terrifying arrangement she had set in place: she was actually proposing that she mess it all up. So she hedged a little. She would just ring Darren and if he wasn't in, then that was it. She wouldn't try anyone else. As the phone rang and rang, her stomach knotted up with hope and fear.

'Hello?' said Darren.

For a moment her throat was too dry for her to speak. 'Hi, it's Esther,' she croaked. 'I need to score.'

'Ah, come on, Esther, you don't want to do that.' He was all blitheness and cheer, meaning he had already scored that day. 'You're doing really well. You don't want to blow it.'

'No. You don't understand,' she said through gritted teeth. 'I do. I've thought about it and that's exactly what I want to do.'

'Well, I'm sorry, Esther, but I can't.' He still wasn't appreciating the urgency of the situation. 'Dee's off now. He was stopping early. He had to pick his kids up or something. He only came out to me as a real favour. And I don't think anyone else is on: it's Christmas, you know. Why don't you wait until tomorrow, see how you feel then? You can give me a call if you still want to.'

She took a deep breath. She didn't want to beg. And although it would have been entirely reasonable to explain to Darren what a stupid, smacked out, selfish arsehole he was, who would have walked every street in south London if she'd had money in her hand and he hadn't yet scored himself, it probably wasn't the moment. She might need him tomorrow.

So instead she said goodbye and put the phone down. That was it, then. The deal had been that if Darren couldn't do it, she wasn't going to. She was even a little relieved. She willed herself to believe that this deal with herself meant something, that it was a binding contract. To ignore the glaring fact that there was no paper, no witness, just herself, alone and free, with no more restraint upon her than a cloud in the sky. It was an appalling thing, this freedom. It cut away the ground beneath her feet.

Trying to blinker her thoughts, she made herself some food and sat down to another evening of television. Towards midnight an old black and white film came on, called *Dracula's Daughter*. In shades of velvet black and pearly, luminous white, a female vampire fought her urge to drink the blood of young women. The soft curve of a neck would awaken her craving. She knew it was wrong; she didn't want to kill them and her guilt tormented her, but sometimes the urge was simply too strong and she gave in to it. A psychiatrist became interested in her case and tried to help her. 'Release,' the vampire pleaded to an unseen God, 'release.' But there was no helping her; her affliction always got the better of her. Her release came only in death.

Esther's legs felt weak beneath her as she left the flat. Outside the night was cold and very quiet. She chose a long route to the late-night shop, which took her past the tiny park and fountain where the most degraded kind of drug users and alcoholics generally hung out. It wasn't on the way to the shop at all, in fact. But for a moment it seemed entirely possible that some junkie would materialise out of the dark winter night and lead her helpfully to his dealer. Or that some unknown dealer would just happen to be waiting around at two in the morning, not to rip her off or try to rape her, but to sell her an honest bag of heroin.

In the shop she bought the packet of cigarettes she didn't need yet and tried to turn herself homewards. But her feet wouldn't do it. She leant on the railings outside the tube station, the metal freezing on to her hands. It was strange to encounter Brixton so quiet; there was hardly a living soul about.

Maybe the film had been right.

She was desperate for heroin. She felt way out of control. If she'd been able to think of any possible way of scoring she would have been there. She eyed up the bus stops and considered King's Cross. It was the only place she knew of at this time of night where there was even half a chance. But for once London's transport system was on her side and even to her deranged mind it was clear that the double night bus ride, besides being unbearable, would actually take so long as to make the plan unfeasible.

How much longer could she go on like this? She walked slowly home again, to the rest of the wakeful night, knowing there was no reason why the next day would be different.

It was the sameness of it that was frightening, that unwavering determination of the mind to find the thing it craves. Whereas a week or so before, in the initial cold turkey, there had been a wealth of variety, a Roman banquet of horrors of the flesh. It was a long time now since a drug project worker had told her it was like a bout of flu. She'd been in for a surprise then, the first time, when instead of a few aches and pains and a runny nose she'd found herself in a torture chamber for two days. But after that she'd known, and maybe that's why junkies dread withdrawal so much: they know what's coming next.

By day two this time it had been getting to her. The pain seemed to come in waves. She kept clenching herself into a ball, trying to squeeze out the gnawing in her legs, but it was right in her bones and she couldn't get to it. Then a minute later it would be her skin that was worse. Her arms and her back were burning. She pulled at the skin on her arms, longing to tear it off. Then the pain in her legs would start shouting for attention again. She turned over and over, trying to find some comfort. The towel she was lying on was soaked with sweat, as wet as if it had been dropped in the bath. It was a thick, sticky sweat, which smelt like something rotten or dead, the worst smell in the world, she was sure. She kept turning over and then over again, she couldn't stop. Her elbows and knees were wearing raw from all her turning, but she had to do it. She had to get away from those awful, gnawing aches.

Spasms of cramp kept gripping her stomach. What if it was bleeding inside and she was bleeding to death? And still she kept retching. She'd drag herself to the edge of the bed, towards the bucket, and vomit up dribbles of water and bile, all food long since gone. Or else she'd feel another bout of diarrhoea coming on and have to trip and stagger to the toilet. Then she'd be back to her soaking wet bed. Attacks of shivers were like razors on her skin. Her teeth were coming loose in her jaws. Sometimes she wondered how long this had been going on. Was it two days now or three? But there seemed to be no way of telling.

And that was it. It was that you had to suffer all this while stranded in a strange and terrifying landscape where all familiarity and safety were dissolved. It was like being lost on the moors, maybe, on a dark, foggy night. Or in the world of a horror film, wandering through graveyards, haunted woods, marshes wreathed in mist, with ghouls and vicious creatures shrieking unseen all around you, always with no idea where you were. You stumbled up to a tree stump or a headstone; it looked like the one you passed an hour ago. Were you losing your mind or were you going round in circles? But the fog was pain and the headstones were the pills you swallowed. Had she taken the last one an hour ago or was it ten minutes? It was impossible to know.

Remembering an old strategy from a previous attempt at kicking, she started noting down which tablets she was taking as she took them. It would have been ironic, to have survived four years of heroin addiction only to die of an accidental overdose of pills.

Sat, 2.00am, 2 x codeine

2.40, 1 x valium

3.15, 2 x sleeping pills

4.05, 2 x sleeping pills

The pen jumped and skidded, a mad person's imitation of writing.

Just a couple of hours' sleep was all she was asking for. She must have been awake for forty-eight hours now. But that was ridiculous. There was no way you could measure this in hours. This was another universe, where hours and days were useless, alien devices.

She took more pills, though why she didn't know. The sleeping pills were pointless over-the-counter things and it was like throwing them down a well. She kept on turning over, the wet covers twisting around her. Her elbows were bleeding, but she couldn't stay still. The pain was eating at the marrow in her legs. In a fit of rage she knelt and pounded the mattress with her fists, but it only sent fire scorching through her shoulders. She put her face into the wet pillow and screamed. The distraction was nice. She screamed again, and again.

She had got herself into something she would never get out of, that much was clear. Two days ago she'd imagined she could do this, but then she'd been on drugs. Whereas now she could see clearly and the fact was, she wasn't going to make it. She had messed around with something she didn't understand. People had warned her, but she'd thought she knew better. She might as well have picked up her life and smashed it on a concrete floor. Now everything good was lost to her. Her life would come to nothing. Instead, just this endless tedium. Working, scoring, working, scoring, all worn out. Hours and days and months spent waiting for dealers who were always late. Trying to shoot up in the mornings when she was sick and shaking so badly it took her an hour to find a vein. Always broke, always owing money, always promising, apologising. Then it would be another job lost. Then they'd finally kick her out of the flat. And sometime it had to come, the overdose or the dirty hit, if it wasn't something slower.

Why had she ever been so stupid?

She took more pills, then more, eking out the codeine with Nurofen Plus and cough mixture, both of them jokes, just mockeries of medicine. All the while illegibly noting down what she was taking, knowing that it was really too much. But if she didn't wake up again, well, why would she be bothered? As long as she could get some sleep.

The glimmer of daylight through the curtains filled her with despair. Another night was over, she wouldn't sleep now. If only she'd saved herself just a little bit of smack, instead of suffering pointlessly like this. She could have weaned herself off gradually, a reducing programme, just like they did in clinics. But maybe there was a way...

She'd dismissed the idea before, thinking there'd be too little on it, but there had to be something left on that last wrap and even the tiniest amount would help.

Clinging to the walls, half on her knees, she reached the kitchen. She was sure it was near the top of the bin. Hunched in pain she lifted the rubbish out piece by piece, inspecting each item for the priceless scrap of plastic. Burnt toast, a biscuit packet, a rotten apple. By halfway down she was genuinely surprised: she really could have sworn it was near the top. With her left arm she hugged her ribs, trying to contain the pain, while with her right hand she lifted out more rubbish. It piled up on the floor beside her. Then right near the bottom her heart leapt. There it was, stuck to a teabag: that little square, cut from a red and white striped plastic bag. She'd been right before: there was almost nothing on it. Just the faintest dusting of brown powder. Plus some ash from the ashtray which had been emptied out on top of it.

Strangely her spoon, the cotton wool and the vitamin C powder were still in their usual place, on top of the chest of drawers. Why hadn't she thrown it all away? But sadly what she had thrown away were her needles. They were all out of harm's way in a yellow sharps disposal bin from the drug project. It was a cylindrical affair with plastic teeth around the top to stop children getting the needles out. She tried to bend the teeth back to shake out a needle, but her finger got trapped and viciously pinched. Tears sprang to her eyes. Frantically she poked around with a biro, but it was useless. Casting her eyes around desperately, she spotted the brick that propped the door open. She put the container on the floor and smashed the brick down on top of it. Pain tore through her fingers, she wondered if they were broken, but the container was still intact. She put the brick on top of it, steadied herself on the chest of drawers and jumped up and down. Finally it cracked. She pulled out a needle. Was it hers or was it Darren's? But this was no time to worry. She'd done worse.

The so-called shot in the needle looked exactly like water. Which was surprising, considering all the cigarette ash. She tried her knee; she'd had a bit of luck there recently. But she was just stabbing dry flesh and the needle felt like it was electrified. Then the back of her forearm, a terrible place at the best of times, where the veins are soft and wobbly. Finally, a squirt of blood in the needle, depressingly clean and scarlet, unmixed with any golden taint of smack.

It was just like injecting a small dose of water.

Then she realised what she should have done all along. She crawled around on her hands and knees, looking for the spot. A couple of weeks ago she'd spilt a wrap on the carpet and there was bound to be some left. She found a smudge of pale powder, but she'd been more efficient in picking it up than she'd imagined. She pushed her face into the synthetic pile and licked. A certain bitter taste told her she had the place, but it wasn't enough to do her any good.

There was nothing for it but to get back into bed. She'd got herself through another half hour; that was all. She clenched herself up tight like a large, stinking, shivering, weeping foetus. How many times had she been through this? She wasn't sure; it was four or five.

She had to remember not to put herself through this again.

Slowly, very slowly the days went by. The next night she got a couple of hours of restless sleep. Gradually the pain subsided to a few dull aches and she was no longer twisting and turning to escape it. To her horror she was overtaken by a frantic sexuality and had to masturbate repeatedly, coming after a minute or two each time. Sexual feelings were not something she'd missed in recent times.

Her friend Julie came round and washed her sheets and towels. She was the first person Esther had seen since she started kicking. Another unwelcome thing to return had been her sense of smell, so she was perfectly aware of how foul everything was, with that stink of kicking that's like nothing else. She was dreadfully ashamed in front of Julie, but too weak and helpless to do anything about it. She sat in a chair wrapped in a blanket while Julie stripped the bed and put a clean sheet on. On the mattress was a dark oval of damp. She felt desperately grateful to her. There was no way she could have done these things herself. Even walking down the corridor to the kitchen she had to stop halfway for a rest. Julie made them both cups of tea and sat with her for a while, keeping her company.

Then Julie left and she felt achingly alone. All emotions were so acute now, she felt like the loneliest person in the world, a lone scientist on an Antarctic station, the last person left on earth after the nuclear blast. On TV she watched a pop music awards ceremony. Before an audience of screaming girls, boy bands and soap stars were honoured for the year. As one winner after another took the stage, it was unbearably moving. She wept uncontrollably.

At night she lay awake until three or four. Giant-sized shadows of terror strode across her darkened landscape. And even in sleep she wasn't safe, because with the return of sleep had come nightmares. As heroin had taken hold of her life, so dreams had ceased, drowned under heroin's treacle sea. In the past few years she had scarcely dreamt at all. Now her subconscious had sprung violently back to life, vengeful and angry from its long suppression. She awoke from the two fitful hours of her third night's sleep struggling to scream. She had dreamt that she was a teenager again, back at home and that somehow her father had moved back in with them. Lying in her bed she had sensed him coming up the stairs, moving up the hall and into her room, a dark, heavy mass without sound or features. As he bent down to kiss her she tried to scream, to squirm away from his descending face. But her body belonged to someone else; she couldn't move. As his lips were about to touch hers, she woke up.

Her face and chest were slimy with sweat. Her heart was thumping against her ribs. She lay still, waiting for her heartbeat to slow, for the heaviness that weighed down her limbs to release her. Why had she been dreaming about her father, of all things, about something that was really nothing? It showed the tricks that kicking played. She resolved to put it from her mind.

The days crawled by and it was nearly Christmas. It had seemed a good time to kick when she'd planned it. It was always difficult scoring then anyway, as dealers took time off and neglected their clients, plus it gave her some extra days off work. She'd phoned in sick on the first day of her kicking, claiming flu. She certainly should have sounded sick enough. Now she wouldn't have to go back until the day after Boxing Day.

But Christmas is a hard time to be alone, and it's a time full of memories. The previous Christmas she had spent alone, too, but she'd been stoned senseless then and she could hardly remember it. It had been a few weeks after Irfan left and she'd been taking no chances: the last thing she intended to have was feelings. But the previous two Christmases had been spent with him. Life had still been pretty good then, him working in the bookshop, her doing layout at the graphics place. They'd got in plenty of gear, plus a little crack for variety, and had passed the time in stoned bliss, baking hot and cosy, nodding out in front of the Christmas TV and having sex on the living room floor.

Her parents had both phoned and she'd lied to them each identically, creating an imaginary Christmas dinner with sprouts and nut roast and pudding, whereas all they'd really eaten were mince pies and most of them they'd puked back up. Irfan's parents had ignored Christmas and phoned a couple of days later.

But now he was gone and there was nothing to shield her from the fact. It was strange: she thought she'd known it well enough. There were still some of his shoes in the wardrobe, the books he'd left behind on the shelf. But he definitely wasn't there beside her in their bed, wasn't in the living room watching cricket for the joy of seeing England lose, wasn't in the kitchen making pizza and a drama. She'd thought this had been evident enough this year gone by.

But when the heroin had begun to leave her body and the world had come flooding back over her sea walls, she was suddenly as floored as if he'd left her yesterday. The last time she'd seen him was as fresh in her mind as a new knife cut, the blood just welling up ready to spill. How he'd just been packing his last few things when she'd decided to go down to Stockwell Park. There had been no need to, really. AJ had said he'd be a couple of hours and for some reason she'd decided she couldn't wait. She'd decided to go and see one of the Jasons, so called by herself and Irfan because they were a small tribe of dealers who all answered the phone to the name of Jason.

'But you know I'm going in half an hour?' said Irfan.

'Yeah. I'll be back.' The door seemed to be pulling her magnetically in its direction. 'It'll only take ten minutes, fifteen at the most. He said he'd be there waiting.'

Irfan hadn't looked convinced. 'Well, be quick. And at least give me a kiss, just in case.'

'No, no, it'll be fine. Look, I'll see you in a minute.'

So she'd left him standing there, looking at her, in the middle of the room. She hadn't given him a last hug or kiss or even said goodbye. She'd just turned and hurried out as if there was something in there she was allergic to. And when she'd come back he'd been gone, as it had been obvious he would be.

She'd hardly shed a tear at the time. Maybe three tears or five altogether, waiting for the tube in the morning or over the hand basin in the toilets at work. But as soon as her kicking kicked in it was like the tears would never stop. They poured out of her eyes like a wet London November, which funnily enough was just what it had been when he left. Not that it had mattered to her then. Now tears soaked her pillow, mixing with her sweat. She howled out loud like a baby for its mother, then suddenly stopped, silenced by the uselessness of it, then started up all over again, crying 'no, no, no,' in disbelief. She awoke from each uneasy stretch of sleep shocked that he was still not there. She missed him so terribly. For the first time she realised that he was gone and it was very likely she would never hold him in her arms again.

CHAPTER 3

The main thing now was time. Esther versus time, this was how the battle was shaping up. But she was at a disadvantage: there was so much more of it than there was of her. She had never seen so much time in her life. It just kept on coming at her. The night before, she had finally got to sleep around five and now here it was, eight in the morning, and she'd snapped awake in a state of emergency. Which was unfortunate, because this was one emergency that could definitely be better faced asleep.

For one thing, she just wasn't used to being awake at this time of day. She'd used to get up this early for work, but then there'd been no time to think about it. It was just a case of getting a shot in her bloodstream and getting out of the door. But on her days off she'd always slept until at least two in the afternoon, as any self-respecting junkie should. She never had to deal with any serious expanses of time by herself.

But now here she was, awake, panic-stricken and exhausted, with the whole terrible day ahead of her. It was like the tide, all this time, masses of it, a flood that nothing could stop. All these huge, wide, hollow hours, gaping like canyons that she was meant to fill. And no longer with drugs, because that was like stuffing tissues in a mouth. Now she was supposed to fill all this time with worthwhile living, with all those things that made up a positive, well-lived life, whatever they were. But the thought of having a whole long life at her disposal opened up a pit of dread inside her. How would she get rid of all that possibility?

The best way to tackle the day seemed to be not to look any questions in the eye. So she tried not to consider the fact that she would normally be fetching a fresh glass of water from the kitchen, lighting her candle and cooking up a comfortable start to the day. Instead there was an unfamiliar need in her stomach which she had to answer with a couple of pieces of toast. Then she had a bath. She was having so many baths these days. They washed off the foul smell which was still oozing through her skin, and they soothed her nerves a little, and best of all they passed some time. Breathing in the smell of lavender, which was meant to have some calming effect, she examined the track marks on her arms and ankles, the sides of her wrists and the backs of her hands. The red of the most recent ones was starting to fade. Some day it would match the white scar of the very oldest, the smooth, flat palette stroke of her first, best vein. She thought of lying back, letting the water close over her face and breathing in.

Her weapon against this morning and its armed squad of hours was to be a trip to a Chinese medicine centre where they did ear acupuncture for problems of addiction. How she'd deal with the afternoon she wasn't yet sure. Maybe she'd have done better to have kept on working, but the day she'd been due back she'd just felt too tired. They'd left a message on her machine asking where she was, but she couldn't face returning it. Then one more message, saying they were cancelling her days, and that was it. She'd have to go and sign on, but she felt too tired to do that either. Maybe she'd feel more capable tomorrow. How easily it happened. She was cut adrift now. If she let herself float away from land, no one would stop her.

Walking down the road towards the acupuncture clinic she felt exhausted and flimsy, as if she could just fall over or be blown away by a gust of wind. How was she going to make it there? It was ten or fifteen minutes' walk (to a normal human being) and she hadn't walked that far since she'd started kicking. It made her want to sit down on the kerb and cry. Everyone was going faster than her. Women with children and pushchairs sped past her. Pensioners zoomed by like sprinters. She felt light-headed; she was frightened she might faint. The cold air cut into her like broken glass. The weak winter sun dazzled her defenceless eyes. Everything was too close: people, dogs, buildings, cars. The pane of glass between herself and the world had been taken away. It was too loud, too bright. It stank: now she could smell again and it was horrible. The world smelt of exhaust fumes, piss, stale beer, dog shit. It was all right in her face. All her senses and appetites were returning at once and it was too much. Why couldn't they arrange to do it more gradually, maybe one by one? Food tasted strong and weird and she had to eat so much of it, she couldn't believe it. She'd been quite happy that she didn't eat much when she was on drugs: not out of any concern to be thinner, but because she just wasn't that taken with the physical world anyway. Now her body demanded to be stuffed with meals at least three times a day and the quantities were astounding. It took up so much time: trying to think of things to eat, buying it, preparing it, chewing her way through it. How did people cope with the boredom?

The clinic itself was hard to find. She went past it at first, peering at various doorways trying to find the right number. Then she doubled back and finally found it, a small, red brick building inside the grounds of a hospital. There was a reception window but no one was there. Inside everyone seemed very purposeful. Through one doorway she could see white plastic reclining beds with people lying on them. In another room people were sitting quietly on rows of chairs, some with their eyes closed, some in strange positions as if they were meditating. Other people were walking busily back and forth, carrying cups of herbal tea and jars of acupuncture needles. She couldn't tell who were staff and who were patients and she had no idea where she should go to get treated. She went back to the reception, but there was still no one there. It was all utterly mysterious. She stood in the hallway again, wondering who to ask. To her horror, she found tears coming into her eyes. She blinked them back.

Gathering all the composure she could, she stopped a young woman in a tracksuit and asked her what she should do to get seen.

'Are you here for five points treatment?'

'I don't know.' Her knees felt as if they'd give way beneath her.

'Ear acupuncture?'

With relief, 'Yes.'

'Right. Well, if you go and sit down through there, in the main room, someone will come round to you.'

She sat down on one of the orange plastic chairs which were lined up in rows. Slyly she checked out the other people. Were they all drug addicts like herself? One young man with shabby clothes and a beard she picked out as a definite. But a middle-aged hippy woman with wooden earrings and a soft pile of grey-streaked hair had her confused. On the walls were anatomical diagrams of the human body marked with acupuncture points, and a black poster inquiring 'Drug Problem?' in large, red letters. Another poster suggested that iridology might be for her. How had she ever come to this? It was a drug comedown all right.

Junkies are an arrogant species. It's a fact not widely known in the world, which is too full of its own conviction that junkies are scum to consider that they in turn might look back upon the rest of society as sad and deluded. Junkies know they are cool because they are doing the best thing a person can possibly do, which is to take heroin. The rest of the world is missing out and the kindest thing would be to pity it, but such is life that people often replace pity with a sneer. And what Esther had particularly liked amid this general certainty of cool was the self-sufficiency with which heroin had imbued her. She hadn't needed anyone or anything else. All she had truly needed was heroin. The rest she could take or leave. And since she generally had heroin, then there hadn't been a problem.

But now, on her plastic chair, begging help from this mystical nonsense, it suddenly occurred to her that she wasn't cool at all. It had all been a lie and the person who'd been fooled most of all was herself.

A man with a bright, wholesome face and a Chinese jade pendant around his neck came and squatted down in front of her. He took an acupuncture needle and stuck it in her ear. Esther winced.

He chuckled. 'Surely you don't mind needles?'

She answered this over-familiarity with a stare.

He put five needles in each ear. They all hurt. He advised her to sit with them in for twenty minutes.

Was it doing any good, she wondered? She'd been told it would calm her nerves, but as the minutes crawled past she couldn't feel any difference. She still couldn't breathe right and her heart was racing along like a train. It was quiet in the room, with just the odd murmur of conversation. Left to itself in this empty time her mind began to wander. To do it with a gun would be good. She could imagine raising it to her temple. It would be nice to get straight to the source of the problem. But she didn't have a gun. Still, there were hundreds of other ways.

As she walked the long, long distance home she reflected that if the acupuncture had done her any good at all it had been hopelessly mild. It was midday now, so that might leave only another twelve hours of the day to go if she was lucky. She lay down on her bed and tried to sleep, but after a few minutes her eyes fluttered open. She felt terribly alone.

CHAPTER 4

They were days and nights spent in heaven, those early times with Irfan. The days started at some luxurious time in the afternoon and the nights went on forever. They lived in a perfect world, just the two of them, complete and whole together, far, far away from the rest of humankind. She had never been so happy with anyone.

They woke up wrapped in each other's arms, the covers spilling off them. Time for a little breakfast in bed, then a chase on some foil and back into each other's arms again. They spent hours and hours making love, slowly crossing changing landscapes, adoring on the plains, ecstatic on the peaks and asleep in the valleys. It was like nothing she had experienced before. They were giddy on the miracle of it, that something like this could have been waiting for them, two people who'd both thought they were on their own. Yet here they were, basking in the heat of it like desert creatures who'd somehow never seen the sun before. Did anyone over all the continents of the earth have the love and joy that they did? It seemed unlikely. No one they knew was as happy as them. They were the luckiest people in the world. Or maybe just the cleverest. It was making them smug, all this bliss. To be celebrating their matchless love in the palace rooms of heroin, it was the best idea there had ever been.

The sex they had together was a revelation. Sex was not something that had meant that much to her before. She hadn't really thought about it at the time, but now it occurred to her that she must have always been a little detached. The sex she had had in previous relationships had looked all right, from some imaginary spot on the ceiling, but she wondered now whether she hadn't just been doing what she thought she should. And then lately it had been changing anyway. In more recent times she hadn't been able to be close to anyone at all: quite literally, she just didn't feel right having anyone intrude upon her space. She had begun to accept that she would have to be alone. She was doing her politics and drinking what she had to to keep things on a level. It wasn't that drinking was so great; it was just that it postponed the arrival of the fact that she didn't know what to do.

And then the last thing she had been expecting: Irfan came along. She had always found him sweet enough, with his nose like a little round bulb and the charcoal shadows around his dark eyes and his intense way of talking about whichever issue of the day was outraging him, waving his hands around as he spoke. But it had never seemed anything to do with her. Then one night in the pub they had started talking and their conversation had gone on all night. She had found herself looking into his eyes a little too long, caught there, unable to look away. The subject of drugs had come up and they'd talked about the hypocrisy which labelled some drugs as good and some as bad.

'The thing is,' said Irfan, 'people just have to think in

dichotomies. They want to prove that the drugs they're taking are good, club drugs and all that, so they have to say that people who take heroin are bad.'

'Exactly!' declared Esther, a little emphatic over her third pint. 'How can a drug be good or bad? It's just a substance. It's what people do with it that matters.'

They talked about the horror that is the ecstasy evangelist, then moved on to other things. At the end of the evening Irfan asked her, 'So what are you doing now?'

Esther stiffened. She wasn't sure this was what she wanted.

Irfan lowered his voice. 'Because I've got a little bit of heroin at home. I don't know if you want to try it…'

An electric shock ran through her. The idea was terrifying. But there was relief in there too: she'd thought for a moment he'd meant sex.

She tried to shrug nonchalantly. 'Yeah, OK. Why not?'

And they sauntered off down the road together, each as cool as the other. There was no way she was letting on how scared she was.

Irfan's flatmate, Mike, another politico, was already there watching TV.

'I don't mention it to him,' said Irfan once they were in his room. 'He wouldn't approve.'

Esther looked around. His shelves, and most other surfaces too, were piled high with books bearing such titles as *A Different Hunger: Writings on Black Resistance* and *Open Veins of Latin America*. One shelf was given over entirely to copies of the journal *Race and Class*. Irfan took a roll of silver foil out of a drawer and tore off two rectangles, then made a crease down the centre of each. He unfolded a scrap of plastic and with the end of a knife put a small spot of sand-coloured powder on one piece of foil and handed it to Esther. Her hand shook as she held it. It was shocking actually to see this stuff that she had heard so much about. Papers and magazines were always full of it, stories of ruined lives and early deaths, all testifying to the unparalleled thrills that heroin must offer.

'Is that all?' she said, offended at the tiny quantity. He obviously considered her some lightweight.

'Yeah, you'll see.' He looked smug. Then he demonstrated the process, running his own foil over a lit candle and sucking up the brown smoke through a tube of foil.

Could she really be doing this? She imitated what he'd shown her. The smoke was bitter in her mouth, unpleasant. She waited, prepared for disappointment. Then a glow lit up in her head like a three-bar heater turning on. She found herself grinning.

'Fucking hell. That's *nice*.'

Irfan smiled. He put some more on his foil and gave her a little more too. She felt sublimely happy. She wasn't sure if it was the drugs or if she was just in a very good mood. A few minutes later she felt urgently nauseous and had to run off to the toilet. She regurgitated a stream of lager and chewed up crisps, but to her surprise it wasn't bad: she could hardly taste it.

Back in Irfan's room they both lit cigarettes.

'Are you glad you tried it, then?' he asked.

She nodded. 'Yeah. Try anything once.' She paused to soak up how very pleasant she felt. 'So do you do it a lot?'

'No, just now and again. I used to. I was addicted to it for a while, for a couple of years. That was a few years back. Then I had to stop and I didn't want to go near it for a while. But now that I haven't got a problem with it anymore, it's nice to do it every now and then, for a treat.'

'Fair enough.' She shrugged. Just because the rest of the world demonised it, that didn't mean they had to, too. She'd never been one to do what she was told and she was proud of that.

'I mean, I know I'll never get really into it again. I just

couldn't. The politics of it are too appalling: where the money goes to, the people it's used against. And when I was really using before, I stopped being active, I stopped doing my writing. They did that in the sixties, in Harlem, flooded the place with heroin to crush the politics that was going on. I don't want to be a part of that, to do it voluntarily, stop myself doing what I should be doing.'

He'd turned all serious. Esther was concerned. 'No. But that's fine, isn't it? You know that now and you're not going to do it again.'

'Yeah.' He pulled a smile. 'You ready for some more?'

And so they went on, talking and talking. She'd never felt so close to a person so easily. The stiffness which normally afflicted her, placing her at a distance from those around her, had melted away. They talked about how they'd got involved in politics: it turned out they'd both been active since their teens. They talked about past relationships and mused over the coincidence that neither of them had been involved with anyone for a while.

'Why haven't you, then?' asked Esther.

'I dunno. I just haven't really felt like it. And I've just been too busy. Well, how about you?'

'Same really. I just started feeling a bit funny about it, I don't know why.'

Esther knew it was getting late, but she was still shocked when she looked at her watch and saw that it was four o'clock.

'I better go.' She got to her feet, still deliciously aware of how light she felt. The world was soft and kind around her.

Irfan stood up too. 'I'll walk you back. You can't walk around at this time of night.'

But she never got as far as the door. Standing there in front of her, it occurred to her how beautiful he was. The curves of his mouth were fine and perfect, but the softness of it still surprised her. Something in her stomach seemed to flip over; she had never felt such a thing before. They kissed for a long time.

Lying face to face it was almost frightening. It was as if there were no barriers between them. Yet she wasn't scared. This unexpected love she felt for him seemed to pour out of her like the sun's rays, with nothing to hold it back. They kissed and touched each other's bodies and fucked for hours, until, around the time his flatmate's alarm clock went off, they both finally came. Still face to face, each tightly holding the other, they fell into a sudden and dreamless sleep.

And as on that first night, so it went on. They had fallen head first into love and there was no going back. Outside it was winter but they didn't care; it was warm as summer where they were. The weekends were the best. Irfan would score on Friday afternoon and from then on they were living like a king and queen. It was the best life imaginable. Esther would hurry home from work and he'd be waiting for her, already stoned, with a neat piece of foil laid out next to the wrap and the candle. They'd make love, then talk, then make love again until the small hours. The next day they'd sleep until late and then start all over again. On Sunday, whoever woke up first would go out for the papers and some pastries for breakfast, then another day in paradise would begin.

And yes, the sex was extraordinary. Neither of them had ever done the things they were doing together, a journey into physical pleasures of every kind that their minds could frame. Their bodies were a playground where love guided their enjoyment, cradling everything they did in immeasurable tenderness. They lived in a land of abundance, where it seemed the fields and orchards of their happiness would never leave them hungry.

But it was much more that. It was the closeness they felt, the conversations which lasted hour upon hour, in perfect intimacy, with no fear to make them keep anything hidden. It was amazing how similar they were.

'It's not that I hate life,' Irfan said one night as they lay on their backs, his arm looped behind her neck. They had been making love, even more stoned than usual, only to fall asleep simultaneously, Irfan lying with his head between her legs, Esther sound asleep on the pillow. When they'd woken up Irfan had made them both peppermint tea, which they drank constantly to try to stop themselves being sick.

He put his mug of tea down to express himself better, his hands leading the way. 'I just hate the way things are. The unfairness of it, the cruelty, the way so many people never have a chance. I can't stand it sometimes. I don't want to make myself some kind of casualty. I know some people might say that with heroin you're getting it all wrong, turning it inwards. But it doesn't have to be self-destructive, does it? It's just . . . maybe sometimes I want a break, from things being the way they are'

'That's it,' said Esther. She tucked a strand of hair behind her ear. 'I like being alive. Well, no, I suppose I haven't always; I do at the moment. Maybe I haven't always felt that enthusiastic about life, but that's because there's so much wrong with it. And I'm not going to pretend it's any nicer than it is; I'd just feel like I was suffocating if I did that. But I don't want to die. I really don't. Why would I want to do that when we're having such a great time together?'

Irfan kissed her. Esther pulled back for a moment and looked into his eyes. She stroked her hand through his short thick hair. Then they started to kiss again.

They marvelled that they had found each other. Irfan played her Indian Qawwali music, a mournful, hypnotic sound which it seemed was the latest thing in leftwing Asian circles. He gave her a present of a book called *India's Simmering Revolution*. She gave him *Patriarchy and Accumulation on a World Scale*.

He told her more about the international politics of the drug trade, how it was the British who had started it at the time of the Opium Wars. 'Right from the start it was a political weapon, you know,' he declared, earnest as ever, one hand cutting the air for emphasis. 'They were doing it partly for the money and partly as a way of just crushing China, because the country was being brought to its knees by the sheer number of addicts there.'

'Well, maybe you could say drugs are the Third World's revenge on the West,' said Esther, no less serious even as her heart leapt out to him. 'Not just for the Opium Wars, but for all of it, the whole set-up.'

'No,' he said, suddenly less spirited. 'No, you can't say that. Because there's too much suffering in the Third World caused by drugs. It's only a few people who are getting rich; it's still the poor who suffer. Do you know how many addicts there are in Pakistan, where all the Afghani heroin gets processed, on its way to Europe? They get all the crap stuff, we get the good quality, the finished product. Besides,' his voice got quieter, 'a cousin of mine, one of my Indian cousins, is in prison for smuggling heroin, in Germany. He got ten years, stuck in prison in a country he doesn't even know, a foreign language, no one to visit him. And for what? So his big-shot so-called friends in the city could write off another loss, which they don't even care about: they expect it, and get some other mug to carry the next lot, for a pittance.'

Esther was silent.

He looked wretched. 'How fucking shit did I feel about that, when I was into it big time? I could never go there again, I'd just feel too bad about it.'

She hugged him. 'No, and we're not going to. We're informed, we know about things. Besides, we've got too much to lose. Of course we're not going to fuck up.'

A flat came up and they decided to move in together. A friend of Irfan's was moving away and offered to pass on his housing association place. As soon as they walked in they liked it. It was on the top floor of a house in a quiet street in Brixton and just the right size. It even had a small study for Irfan to do his writing in. He had a blue notebook which he carried everywhere with him to make notes in for his poetry; now he'd be able to work at it in peace. In the bedroom the light filtered in through the new spring leaves which were just forming on the trees in the garden.

'It's got a good vibe,' said Esther. 'It feels like a place where we'll be happy.'

Neither of them had ever lived with a lover before and they'd only been together a few months, but it was hard to have any doubts. The day they moved in they should have been tired. They'd been at Irfan's place the night before, sitting on the bed amid the bags and boxes of his belongings, waiting for the dealer until late. They'd both agreed that moving house was something which would be better undertaken with the benefit of drugs. Why suffer needlessly? There had been some big raid somewhere which meant there was virtually nothing around, but Steve had said he'd be able to get some. He was driving out to the south coast and Irfan kept getting progress reports from his girlfriend on the phone.

'Ugh, she says she's sick,' said Irfan with a shudder. 'Such a horrible thought.'

It tore at Esther's heart when he said things like this. It was strange and terrible to imagine him like that, a sick junkie needing a fix. She was used to having a hangover and sore eyes on a Monday, a few aches around her teeth, but the idea of true withdrawal was like something from a horror film, a world far removed from reality.

Steve had finally shown up around one in the morning, which meant they'd had four hours sleep when the van came the next day. They lugged all the boxes up the stairs, then went back to Esther's place to fetch her stuff, and the effort didn't bother them at all. In the flat they walked from room to room, delirious that it was theirs. They hung a blanket over the bedroom window and made love on the bare mattress on the floor.

Setting up home together was like a game: they were pretending to be like any other couple, but of course they weren't. They were like any happy couple but cleverer. They went into town to buy fabric for curtains, high partly on drugs and partly on the sheer outrageous fact of it. They were doing what everyone said couldn't be done and they were getting away with it, like some fantastic tight-rope act, high above the ground and sparkling in the lights, with the roar of applause down below. The fabric they chose was a beautiful sea green, like underwater emeralds. Irfan said his mother had a special occasion sari the same colour and Esther felt proud to be with him, someone different from the ordinary, dull English. All it needed was to be sewn into curtains. They hung it up at the windows, tucked over the curtain rails, just to make do until they could get round to it.

Out on the streets they looked good together. They were the same height, a similar build. She was tall for a woman, he was slender for a man. Her straight back and narrow hips gave her an androgynous quality; his large, dark eyes and delicate mouth were pretty, almost girlish. They got a lot of looks, maybe for being different races, maybe for the shared halo of arrogance which said they were breaking still more rules than that. They were walking on air in those days, sorry for all the people who weren't them.

Irfan got given a number for someone called Jimmy, who turned out to be the nicest dealer in the world. He was caretaking a friend's business while he was 'away' and seemed not to have read the rule book which declares that dealers must be unreliable on a good day and plain psychotic on a bad one. Instead, he delivered direct to their door with no complaints and if he was so much as five minutes late he'd apologise and promise not to let it happen again.

Irfan showed her how to shoot up. He tied the cord of her dressing gown gently around her arm and stroked and patted at the soft part just below the elbow where the veins are open and vulnerable.

'You've got good veins,' he said. 'You've got the right build. Kind of lean.'

The needle hurt just a little as it went in. She had never imagined in her life that she'd be doing this shocking thing. A moment later a surge of electricity filled the inside of her head. It wasn't like sex; it was better. Then it buzzed more gently through her body, spreading down towards her hands and feet. She was getting away with it again, swimming naked in this illicit joy which the rest of the world said mustn't be touched. But they were right and the rest of the world was wrong.

The living was good. Esther was working at the design company and Irfan was at the black bookshop. She liked her work, laying out adverts, posters, brochures as the designers specified. There was something wonderful about typesetting and graphics, a discrete world with its own laws and system of measurement running parallel to the more earthly one of gravity and miles and pounds and ounces. It was a world of potentially perfect order, in which, with enough care and attention, the style of every word and letter in any given job could make irreproachable sense. And Irfan was happy in his work, too, for the contact and involvement it gave him, as the bookshop served as a meeting place and postal address for countless groups from Turkish Marxists to Colombian political refugees. There were plenty of collective meetings bidding to keep him locked away in smoky rooms late into the night, but Esther never had cause for complaint: he always hurried home to her and often skipped them outright. Their world was too magical for him to miss more than a moment.

In her spare time she was supposed to be working on *What She Wants*, a feminist magazine whose strapline gave its aim as 'the overthrow of civilisation as we know it' – it had always seemed a reasonable enough plan to her. She'd been part of the founding collective and for three years had poured into it every spare drop of her energy. Likewise Irfan was allegedly involved in the setting up of a radical Asian theatre group in the East End and, judging from the messages on their answerphone, its other members still believed he was. But somehow neither of them was putting in the hours they intended. It was no wonder, though. All the fun they were having together was keeping them busy, that and just plain happiness.

But now it was just her left alone in their flat. She wondered from time to time whether she shouldn't clear out some of his things. Maybe then she'd feel less like she was smothering in memories, more like there was a new life ahead of her.

Today was another cold day in Brixton. She'd already been for ear acupuncture and later she was planning a trip to the drug project to pick up some more herb tea, but she was saving that a while. She couldn't use up all her day's excitement in one go. So maybe this was the time to do it. After *Neighbours* had finished, of course.

A lot of his possessions were still in cardboard boxes, where they'd been ever since they first moved in. They'd always meant to get round to unpacking properly. Then he'd added to these when he went away, a couple more boxes of things he couldn't carry and didn't want to throw away, a couple of bags in the bottom of the wardrobe. She had no idea when he'd be back to pick it all up.

She pulled a bin liner out of the wardrobe and peered inside. It seemed to be full of winter clothes: she could see a couple of jumpers, some dark trousers. Memories flew out of the bag like startled birds. Irfan with his legs up on the sofa, a roll-up in his hand. The two of them on a freezing, dark afternoon shopping in Camden market. The warmth of his belly underneath his T-shirt.

He must have thought he wouldn't need these things. Maybe she should take the whole lot to Barnardo's, but what if he was cold, what if he needed it? Or there might be some favourite item he'd forgotten. She dragged a box into the middle of the room instead. A cloud of dust flew up from the lid as she opened it. Inside it was full of papers. There were letters, diaries, old political newspapers turning yellow. More old years leapt up to meet her. On top of the pile was his little blue poetry notebook. She couldn't believe he hadn't taken it. It seemed like prying, but all the same she took it out and opened it. On the first page was a column of words. In Irfan's neat, forward-slanted writing it said:

bread
onions
peanut butter
baked beans
marg
washing-up liquid

She turned the page. The same again:

tinned toms
biscuits
bread
cornflakes

tea bags
soap
spaghetti

A few more lists like this, then the rest of the book was blank.

It was no good. She was too tired to decide what to do with this stuff. She put the bag back in the wardrobe and pushed the box back against the wall. She'd have to do it another time.

CHAPTER 5

Irfan had gone and her heart was broken.

And every day there was still all this time. It was relentless. It wouldn't go away and it wouldn't go any faster. It just kept dragging along at the same miserable pace. The struggle of getting through it was like climbing a rock face. Each hour was like fumbling with her toes for each new foothold, like searching out the next grip for her hands. It was that difficult, that strategic, that frightening. And all the time her mind was throwing stones at her as she clung on high above the ground, saying heroin, heroin, heroin. That it was the finest thing a person could do; and if it wasn't good, it was inevitable.

And to make it worse, she was so damned lost. She had no idea what coming off heroin was meant to be like. Beyond the notorious torture of cold turkey, she knew nothing about it. She'd never seen it in any film or book, never talked to anyone who'd done it. How long did it take to get better? Had anyone else ever felt what she was feeling? Or was she just a hopeless case? She was all at sea with neither map nor stars to guide her. Forced to go begging to strangers for help.

Standing at the bus stop, her friend Nicky tapped her on the arm. If 'friend' was the word.

Nicky peered into her face. 'You're looking...' she hesitated, '*well.*'

'Uh huh,' said Esther dubiously. It seemed unlikely. Back at the flat she'd looked deathly pale and tired enough for a hospital bed. Then she understood: Nicky was using 'well' in the sense of 'not stoned out of your mind'.

She decided to concede the point. 'Yes, I am well, thank you.'

At the drug project she sat down in the drop-in room to wait for someone to see her. Various junkies sat around drinking tea, also waiting their turn to be seen. A couple of voluntary workers kept them company, a tattooed man in his forties and a bright-eyed young black woman. In her experience the volunteers divided down the middle into ex-drug users and student social workers.

'How many sugars?' the older man boomed jovially.

'Just one.' She smiled. The sweet tooth was taken for granted.

Meanwhile the other clients, as they were doggedly termed by the project, had raised themselves to a little light conversation.

'The thing is,' said a sweet-faced young hippy girl, 'I just like drugs.'

'Yeah, so do I,' said a man with a shaved head and waxy, pale skin. He sounded surprised, clearly struck by the coincidence.

'Yeah, so do *I*,' said another man, nodding his head in amazement. 'I mean, it's just a hedonistic thing, isn't it? We like having a good time.' The crutches at his side and his fat, bandaged foot testified to the earnestness of his quest for fun.

'OK?' said one of the project workers at her side. She had dyed red hair and bags under her eyes. She looked as tired as Esther felt.

'I just...I just wanted to talk to someone,' Esther mumbled towards the floor. It had been easier when all she needed from this place were new needles.

'All right.' The woman nodded to a corner of the room where they'd only be overheard by a few people.

Trembling pitifully and looking at her shoes, Esther explained why she was there. 'So, I mean, it's been a month now,' she finished up. 'Do you, do you think I should still be feeling like this?' She met the woman's eyes, looked away. 'Do you think it's... normal?'

'Well, it does take a while for things to settle down, you know. You were using for a while; you don't just get over it overnight. But it's different for everyone, really. Have you thought of getting some counselling? There are probably things you should be dealing with. It might help.'

'Oh, I don't know about that.'

'You've got nothing to lose. Why don't you give it a try?'

'Well, I could...' Somehow her skills of discouragement were failing to work on this woman.

'OK, then. I'll book an assessment for you. It'll be in a couple of weeks.'

Esther smiled and nodded, trying to look appreciative, but she was disappointed. Why couldn't she give her a straight answer? She just wanted to know when she'd be better. And she couldn't help thinking she was on the wrong track with this counselling idea. Nothing terrible had ever happened to her; her life had been perfectly ordinary. The obvious fact was that there was something wrong with her brain. She had been born wrong and the only question was how it had taken her so long to notice.

Before she left, one of the volunteers gave her another bag of herbal tea. 'Thanks,' she said politely, but she felt sorry for them. They were clearly only handing out this stuff to make themselves feel better about the fact that they had nothing useful to give away, like proper medicine.

She waited for the bus back up Stockwell Road, an ant following its own tracks, her life made up of tiny journeys back and forth.

Nothing was any clearer. She was still just as lost as before.

Lucia came down from Hackney to visit her and Esther was ashamed of how much she needed her company. She had been watching the clock all morning, counting down the hours.

'That fucking bastard,' said Lucia as soon as she was inside the door. 'I hate him so much, I can hardly describe it.' She kissed Esther on both cheeks and they walked through to the kitchen, where Esther put the kettle on. Suddenly she wished she'd bothered to get changed out of her dressing gown. Lucia was dressed in a slim-fitting charcoal-grey woollen jumpsuit. Her thick, dark hair swung glossily around her tiny, pretty face. Esther realised how grubby the flat had become.

'He came round this morning, asking for that money I owe him,' Lucia continued. 'Just arrived on my doorstep, like he's got that right! "Oh, hello, Lucia. I've come to get that money." Fucking bastard. I told him he has no right to any damn money, the way he treated me. Fucking pig. It's him who should be giving me money, for the pain and misery of having been in that relationship with him. Why am I so stupid! I thought, oh yes, English men, no way can they be so bloody awful like Italian men. English men, they know feminism, at least they aren't Catholic, can't be so damn ignorant and bad in bed, besides, as Italian men. Well, ha ha, how stupid I am. That is my lesson for being in relationships with men. I must be crazy. What other reason is there to continue with it?' She took a breath, then confided more happily, 'I was so angry, though, to see him. He tried to come in through the door, so I kicked him.

In the leg. Then shut the door. I don't think he'll come back again so quickly.'

Esther smiled back at her. They were in the living room now, cups of coffee in their hands, which Esther had made especially for her guest, Lucia's handbag on the sofa beside her. It was good to have a messenger from the living world outside. Sometimes she forgot it still existed.

'But anyway, Esther, how are you, my dear? Is it OK? Are you getting better? You look a little pale.'

'I dunno,' answered Esther. Her voice suddenly felt feeble, perhaps from lack of use. She grabbed her cigarette packet. 'I'm not sure if this is working. I still don't feel right, you know?'

'Uh huh.'

She tucked a strand of hair behind her ear, tried to smile, but her voice had dropped almost to a whisper. 'I'm sure it's not meant to be like this. I still can't sleep. I'm in a panic all the time. I really don't feel right in the head.' She gave a little laugh. 'Maybe I'll just have to be sedated all my life.' She shrugged, or at least tried to. 'Might as well be a drug addict, really.'

The room went quiet for a moment. Esther wondered whether Lucia could hear her heart beating; it sounded deafening.

Lucia shook her head firmly. 'No, come on, Esther, don't say that. You know you're a strong person. You're doing really well.'

Esther dragged on her cigarette, looked at the wall, tried to steady her breathing. 'Have you ... have you ever known anyone who managed to do it?'

'To stop taking smack?'

Esther nodded.

'Oh, well, I don't know for sure. There was a lot of it back home, you know. Maybe it was a difficult place to clean up. I knew some people, a few of them, who tried. Maybe it's not a good example ... And here in London, well ... But anyway, that's not important. We know it's a hard thing, that's why it's hard for you now. But you are going to do it, because you're determined, so you will.'

Esther nodded again. 'Right.'

'And you know, I'm sure you could get something from the doctor to help you,' Lucia continued. 'Sleeping pills or how is it called? Tranquillisers. Something to calm you. Why don't you go to see the doctor? It's because you can't sleep that you're feeling so bad. If you get some pills you'll feel better.'

Esther nodded once more, this time with more enthusiasm. This sounded like good advice. Why hadn't she thought of it herself? 'Yeah, you're right. I'll make an appointment. I'm sure that'll do the trick.' She felt a glow of love for Lucia, her old, dear friend.

After she'd gone the flat seemed desolately empty. She sat in the kitchen and lit another cigarette. The clock ticked loudly on the wall and the fridge hummed. The aching loneliness in her chest was like the weight of a stone, trying to choke out her breath. It occurred to her that Lucia's positivity was a wonderful thing; it was just nothing to do with her. It was nonsense to think that she could change her life from the limping, sick creature it had become into some kind of sunny field. She was a born junkie: that was the truth of it. Her place was on the other side of the mirror, the world of darkness and destruction. Strength, health and happiness might sit fine with other people, but they weren't for her. She tried to imagine what it might be like to make them her goals, to strive for a long life, packed with good things like the seeds in a pomegranate, but the leap of mind was too great. She wasn't like that.

Something somewhere had shifted in her worldview. Once she had seen herself as an agent of change, something outside the wrongness of the world which could catalyse it for the better, but now she couldn't remember how to think that way.

Now she wondered if it was even right, to try to save herself in this messed up, awful world. How could she save herself when others would be left behind? To do anything else but destroy oneself seemed morally dubious. Really the best thing now would be to go out and score.

But the next day she felt different. She had made her doctor's appointment, though it wasn't for a few days yet, but it wasn't just that. It was just that it struck her how wonderful it was not to be on drugs anymore. She was clear-headed: she could think straight and it was amazing. Her head was no longer wrapped in a fog which put the world out of reach, distant and uncertain. Yes, her nerves were twanging with panic day in, day out, but at least it was a sign of life. It was a whole month now since she'd started kicking: surely she had cracked it. She wasn't going to spend her life a drug addict after all. She was going to have a life! It was extraordinary news. She was no longer chained to that insistent, regular demand which meant she had to cook up a dose of poison every few hours, no longer had to put a shot in her veins first thing in the morning just to push away the sickness and pain she woke up with. She had dragged herself out. She had done it: she was free.

And soon she'd get a prescription from the doctor. It was bizarre that she hadn't thought of it sooner; it had just made things needlessly difficult. Maybe the doctor would give her valium for the daytime and temazepam to get to sleep. It would make sense to have both. To think, in the past she'd paid good money for illicit supplies of these things. Now she'd be getting them for free. Then she'd stop feeling so terrible, the drug cravings would pass as well, she'd gently wean herself off the pills and everything would be fine. It was such a relief.

But as she contemplated the next three days before the appointment she felt her mood plummet, a bird shot dead in mid-flight. It was a rollercoaster ride this, it couldn't be denied. Three days full of long, long hours, and she'd had to trick away so many hours already. Maybe she'd get valium from the doctor and she'd have to take it for the rest of her life. Whenever she tried to stop, she'd feel the same as she did now. Previously she'd drunk, then she'd taken heroin. There was just something wrong with her. Nothing had changed to make it different now.

She lay down on her bed to try to think. What was she going to do? It was a constant refrain through the days now, this question. What was she going to do? The ceiling spun and wavered.

She fought her way through a couple more days. Quiz shows, talk shows, cookery shows, black and white films, kids' TV. As the chef demonstrated aubergine puffs she daydreamed of getting a quarter and shooting up the lot. Surely that ought to be enough, now that she was clean. But it seemed unsatisfactory. It didn't seem right to be dead and know nothing about it. It wasn't what she was looking for.

She made her fortnightly trip to the dole office and signed her name without a word spoken. The absurdity of swearing that she was fit for work could have made her laugh in better times.

At night she clutched a pillow to her chest to pretend she wasn't alone. The minutes and hours inched towards morning. At seven o'clock she awoke exhausted from a dream in which she was a stranger who had murdered herself, Esther, with an axe to the back of the neck, then chopped up her body and buried it in a Fenland ditch under smoke-black skies. But first she had pulled the teeth from her freshly dead gums and chopped off each finger tip, so that the body would remain forever unknown.

She'd have been in good company. Irfan had told her that in

Victorian times, when the country dosed itself regularly on pennyworths of opium, it had been most popular of all in the Fens, where chemists did a roaring trade on market day and local brewers even put it in their beer.

But at least this hell was nearly over.

'How long have you been feeling like this?' the doctor asked.

'For, like, a month or so. It's just, I've been going through a relationship break-up, so I just think I might need something to kind of tide me over.' She tried to meet her eyes, not to look like she was lying. She had never sought help from the medical profession for her drug use before and saw no reason to forsake her privacy now.

'Right,' the doctor nodded. 'Well, I think you're maybe rushing things a bit. It's natural to feel this way. It's never easy coming to the end of a relationship, we all find it hard.' She gave Esther an understanding look, sadly misplaced. Then the body blow: 'I think you'd do better to wait it out.'

On the wall behind the doctor's head was a poster of children's drawings: a parade of felt-tip peacocks. Everything had frozen up. Or rather, time was still moving, but Esther had got trapped. She couldn't think. 'No. I mean, I really can't sleep. I feel all panicky all the time. I've tried to wait, but I can't.' What was it she should say?

'These are strong medicines. It's much better not to rely on them.' The doctor was calm and firm. 'If you don't feel better in a few weeks you can come back and we'll talk about the options again.'

A few weeks? She could be dead by then.

There was no point protecting herself anymore. 'The thing is, I've been coming off heroin, but it's been quite hard.'

'My, you have been going through a lot. So you've done this by yourself?'

'Yes.'

She raised her eyebrows. 'Well, that's good going. But I'm still going to say the same. Tranquillisers and sleeping pills are addictive. That's why we don't like giving them out.'

'Not as addictive as heroin,' said Esther quietly, before she could stop herself. If she'd been older or looked more respectable she'd have got temazepam, no trouble. They dished it out to old ladies all the time.

'Sure. Well, look, if things don't work out, we can maybe think about putting you on methadone.'

The doctor's last shred of credibility was gone. Esther was filled with contempt. Why would she go through the hell of coming off one opiate only to go onto another, more addictive one instead? Did they teach these people nothing?

But her sneer faded before it had begun. Insane as it might be, the terrible fact was that she was at this woman's mercy. She was falling now, down and down into a pit the bottom of which she couldn't see. Flailing for something to hold on to.

It had gone quiet in the little surgery room.

'Please,' said Esther.

The doctor sat back, folded her arms. 'I'm sorry.'

What if she just threw herself down on the carpet in front of her and begged? Or refused to leave the surgery until they gave her something?

Instead she got up stiffly and left the room without a word. Outside on the street the tears poured down her face. She hadn't been prepared for this; it had never occurred to her that this might not work. She was in trouble now.

Back at the flat she closed the front door behind her. She had no idea how she'd got there. She slid to the floor and leaned her back against the door. Fear had reduced her thoughts to a single phrase: I mustn't score. As if this piece of driftwood would keep her afloat. I mustn't score. There was no point wondering why she mustn't, because she didn't know. It was just something she remembered had once been true.

It would be so beautiful to put a needle in her arm.

A whirlwind had taken off in her head, spinning debris around in a thick, murky swirl, which was why she couldn't see anything clearly anymore. If only there was someone else around. Then they might know what to do, because she herself had no idea at all.

In the sitting room the light was flashing on her answerphone. She pressed the button and her mother's voice crackled out: 'Hello, Esther, it's your mum here. Just phoning to see how you are. Oh well, looks like I've missed you again. Give me a ring sometime...'

The sound of her voice, the way it jarred with this here-and-now, increased the static in her head.

Her fingers dialled a more familiar number. After a few rings, Lucia's answer machine came on. 'Hi, sorry we're not in. Please leave a message...'

How could she explain? It seemed impossible to work out. She put the receiver down and sat staring at it. Was there anyone else she could call? This seemed impossible to work out as well. She lay down on the floor where she was and curled herself into a little ball. Perhaps this way she could protect herself. Should she be lying here, on the living room floor, or would another spot be better? Maybe she should get into bed. But the journey down the hall seemed too dangerous. So many questions, all of them too hard for her. Maybe she should be drinking, just knock out her consciousness, but the shops were like the other side of the world. She had to find some way of stopping this.

But it had become impossible to step from one thought to another. She pushed herself to her feet and made her way to the bedroom, leaning against the wall to steady herself. In a drawer was the yellow plastic needle holder, which she'd smashed open when she was kicking. Must get round to throwing that out, she laughed to herself, a little joke.

She tied up, just above the knee, sucked the point clean and aimed the empty needle for where the vein used to be. It took a few tries, but she'd gone numb, it didn't hurt. Then she slowly drew the plunger back. Her blood in the barrel was scarlet and lovely, as beautiful a thing as she had ever seen. It made a bright pool in the palm of her hand. As she washed it over the back of her other hand, then back over the first, it coated them like red gloves. It was surprising how strong the colour was. She pushed up her sleeves and smeared some up the inside of her forearms. It was nice to see it there, though it was getting darker and dryer now, less slippery. It reminded her of how much time she'd spent contacting the blood that flowed there beneath the skin.

Then she'd run out, so she had to go back for another needleful. A trickle of blood had run down her leg from the first time round. Looking in the mirror, she stroked red onto her cheeks. She noticed that she was crying: her face was wet with tears, which watered down the colour. She took her sweatshirt and vest off and painted blood down her chest.

Then she started to sob in earnest, because she realised she was going to die and it was so sad. She covered her mouth to stifle gasps of shock. To think, she'd been alive, she could have had a whole, long, proper life, but it wasn't going to work out. She remembered herself as a little girl and it occurred to her that she must have been a sweet child, serious but sweet. She could picture herself playing in her favourite checked dress, which she wore and wore until it was far too small and only relinquished when the zip burst at the back. She and her two best friends had used to play in the waste ground behind her house, exploring among the rubble and the thistles and the thick, sweet smell of lilac bushes. How had things turned out so wrong?

And she felt so sorry for her mum and her brother. That set her crying all the more. It was such a terrible thing to happen to them. But there seemed no way to avoid it.

She'd never thought it would happen like this. All this time she'd been both hoping for it and fearing it and she'd thought it would be quite different. She'd imagined that if it ever did come to this, it would be because one day she'd weigh things up and decide, in some cerebral way, that she had no chance of a happy life. And here it was overtaking her in a rush and a turmoil, her head all thick and messy, with no chance to stand back and enjoy it.

She'd have to cut her wrists, there was no doubt about that. Anything else seemed too blunt or too messy or too oblivious. She knew it was a bad way of doing it, that if someone found you they just dragged you off to hospital and sewed up your wrists and there you were, alive and furious. But the idea of her body all mangled up as she hit some piece of pavement was all wrong. Or a rope burning her neck in a thick, red stripe. Or writhing and screaming as the bleach burnt through her stomach. No, she wanted to be herself, whole and awake, stepping out on her way to death. With just one final, celebratory show of blood.

Besides, there was no danger of anyone finding her.

But it seemed wrong as well to die alone, without the company of heroin. If she was going to die, she should make it right: she was only going to do it once. Once heroin had been about heaven, the only heaven she believed in. A pure, unearthly peace and joy that raised her up skywards with just her toes pointing down towards the ground. Surely this was the condition of mind in which she should take her last happiness.

She would have one last hit, a good one, just as strong as a good hit should be and no stronger, and that would be the end of it.

All she needed was to score and buy some razors.

Then she started to cry again. She could see now what had happened. She fumbled her way into the living room and pulled out the phone book. Who did you call about these things? She had no idea. The police station, maybe. Was that it? Her eyes slid over the list of emergency numbers at the front but none seemed right. On the back cover was an advert for Childline. At least they could advise her.

It was a man's voice, far away at the other end of the line.

For a moment she felt human again and her throat was too choked up to speak.

'I, I think I've gone mad. I need to find out how to section myself.'

'Why do you think you've gone mad?'

'Because... I can't look after myself anymore.'

'Uh huh. How do you mean, exactly?'

Again she couldn't speak. The futility of it had taken her voice. This man could have been on Mars, he was so far away.

'Hello? Are you still there?'

'Oh, sorry.' She jerked back into wakefulness. He sounded old; maybe he was doing this because he was bored in his retirement. But she began to explain while he listened. It was hard, there seemed so much to it, and it was embarrassing, too, to be so crazy.

'Listen,' he said, with a certainty that surprised her. 'You really shouldn't section yourself. It'll only make things worse. You've just got to try to hold on through tonight, then phone a proper drugs helpline in the morning. I'll give you some numbers, because we're more a phoneline for children, you know?' This part was said tentatively, as if she was too demented to know who she'd phoned.

But how could he judge so quickly that she wasn't insane? It seemed a snap diagnosis. The tears started out down her cheeks again, silently. Why wouldn't he let her give up? It was just too much. She wanted to be allowed to give up.

The next day, cold and very early, she awoke to find the bed dusty with crumbs of dried blood. She was tired to the bone. In the mirror her face was swollen and puffy. It seemed strange that things could look so ordinary. But at least she knew what to do. If it was a choice between suicidal madness and taking heroin, it was clear enough which she'd have to pick. She turned on the early morning TV and lay on the sofa to wait, while the clock in the corner of the screen told her exactly how slowly the minutes were rising.

She got to Darren's about elevenish and banged on the door until he opened it, bleary eyed with a sheet wrapped around him.

'For God's sake, Esther? What is it? Some kind of national emergency?'

She managed a tiny smile. 'Yeah, something like that.'

He stood back to let her in, then followed her down the hallway. 'Have you got any money?'

'No, but you can get credit.'

Darren started to pout. 'You know Dee hates that . . .'

'And how much do you owe me?'

He scowled, then turned away. Leaving her in the kitchen to make tea, he disappeared into the bathroom for twenty minutes, but Esther wasn't tempted to bother him. She needed something better than the yellow cottons he was no doubt cooking up.

'And you know he never starts before midday,' he complained when he emerged.

Esther smiled and shrugged. Just the thought of medication

had calmed her. Her intention was propelling her forward like a torpedo from a warship. Whys and wherefores couldn't keep up with her.

'Well, it's lucky I'm still using,' he informed her, 'or what would you do then?'

'It's very considerate of you.'

'Yeah, well, I have to anyway, you know I do. I'm getting housed because I'm a drug addict. Those flats are specifically for addicts. I've got to keep taking drugs or I won't be able to get one.'

'Mm hmm.' She nodded. Nothing mattered because soon she would be stoned.

Darren kept hitting redial every five minutes until Dee's phone came on. Esther laid everything out ready on the coffee table so that she wouldn't have to waste a second when he arrived: a fresh glass of water, a brand new needle supplied by Darren, a spoon from the kitchen resting neatly on a square of toilet paper so as not to make a mess with the soot.

Darren pulled some clothes out of a bag and modestly stepped into the hall to get dressed. Perhaps in celebration of Esther's company, he picked out a full-length A-line floral print skirt, though after that it seemed he'd run out of energy, since it was matched with his usual khaki sweatshirt, socks and battered trainers.

Esther considered, as she often did, how little suited his physique was to women's clothing. He was at least six feet tall, with strapping shoulders and hands like baseball gloves. His nose was slightly squashed from a fight in his youth, which never seemed to help his attempts at wearing make-up.

'Seen any more of that whatsername?' Esther asked.

'Natalie. No. I don't think she was... really interested.'

'That's a shame. You know, maybe it would be better just to wear blokes' things when you go out. Let them get to know you first, then kind of introduce the idea gradually.'

'Yeah, I s'pose. It's just, you know, it's hard. I want to look nice when I'm out somewhere...'

But then the doorbell rang and nothing else mattered to either of them anymore.

If someone had asked Esther what good she thought this was going to do and whether she was aware that the next day or the day after that she'd be back exactly where she was now, only a little worse, she'd probably have admitted that she knew it perfectly well. It wasn't as if her options had changed. Nothing new had come into the picture. She would still have to wake up sick and face the choice between returning to addiction, which was unbearable, or trying to go forwards without drugs, which was almost equally unbearable.

The wonderful advantage of heroin, though, is that it takes the obvious and puts it somewhere else.

'Be careful,' warned Darren. 'You know you're clean now. I don't want you dying on me.'

'So call an ambulance,' said Esther.

But an overdose would only have been a side effect.

The hit was a better one than she'd had for a long, long time. And then the absolute, magical relief of everything switching off.

CHAPTER 6

The first time Irfan OD'd Esther thought it would make a difference.

They were in the living room, which was where they usually cooked up. They'd both got in from work at the same time, fretted and fidgeted until Jimmy came round. Irfan found a vein faster than she did: the advantage of being a bloke. He took the needle out and untied.

'Bloody hell, have you done it already?' she complained, still prodding around, putting a little backwards pressure on the plunger to see if any blood came up. 'How is it?'

The news was on, a story about a young girl and her mother, both found murdered together.

'Don't answer me, will you?' She turned to look at him. His eyes were closed. For a moment he stayed upright in the armchair, then he started to sag forwards, as if someone had cut the strings which held him upright.

She caught him just before his head hit the coffee table.

'Speak to me! What's the matter?' She tried to shake an answer out of him, but his head just flopped around sickeningly. For a moment her mind refused to accept it.

Confused knowledge came back to her, from magazines, books, rock'n'roll stories. She patted his cheek. Shouted: 'Irfan! Irfan!' Slapped a little harder. 'Irfan! Wake up!' He kept sliding forwards. He was strangely heavy. She pushed him back again; he slid over sideways. She slapped him harder still. Nothing. Shouted as loud as she could: 'Irfan! Irfan! Irfan!'

She picked up the glass of water they'd used to cook up with and threw it in his face. Still nothing. He just lay there, slumped on his side. She ran into the kitchen for more water. A stream of words was pouring from her mouth, 'No, no, no, no,' as if by will alone she could refuse this. An echo of her words came back to her, weird and disembodied, an imitation of her voice, which itself was an imitation of some overblown scene in a film. His T-shirt was soaked, but it had made no difference. For a second she stopped still, frozen and helpless.

His lips were a purplish blue. His face had changed too, from brown to a strange plum colour. Was he dead already? It wasn't possible. To have slipped out of her hands so quickly.

She wouldn't allow it. She would fight her way backwards through the tidal wave of time to undo this.

She snatched up the phone and dialled, the number like a kids' prank or a crime story on TV. 'Ambulance, please.' Still acting a part. Waiting to be connected, her voice in the earpiece still saying 'No, no, no.'

'Heroin overdose.' It was such a weird thing to say. It made her sound like someone else. She gave the address and hung up.

What if he was choking on his tongue? She'd heard of that somewhere. She forced his mouth open and stuck her finger in past his teeth, tried to push the tongue flat. Was he dying now because she didn't know how to save him? She put her cheek up to his mouth, but couldn't tell if he was breathing or not. Tried to feel for a vein in his neck, couldn't tell if there was a pulse. He still looked like the person she loved. Still looked like the person she'd been talking to a moment before. Was she meant to believe that the difference between dead and alive could be such a tiny sliver of time? It didn't make sense. But what if it was true? What would she do if she was left stranded in this world alone? It would all be useless to her without him.

The ambulance had its siren on. She was surprised in a way: treating them like normal people who deserved this kind of effort. She ran downstairs and out into the street, then led the paramedics upstairs. There were two of them, a man and a woman. The man was carrying a toolbox of equipment.

Seeing them in the living room it suddenly hit her how sordid it looked. The coffee table had got knocked over as she'd tried to push Irfan upright. The floor was a mess of spoons, needles, spilt glasses, candles. Everywhere she looked there was junkie paraphernalia, as if it had dropped down out of the sky. What on earth would they think?

The paramedics were fast. They moved together like two parts of a machine. Out of nowhere they were suddenly trying to put a needle in his arm.

'Is he going to be all right?'

The woman looked at her for a moment. 'I don't know.'

Esther stood watching them, trying to understand. But she couldn't. None of it was possible. Then she realised they were trying to use a vein that Irfan had given up on. She bit her lip, embarrassed by her knowledge.

'I don't think you'll be able to do it there.' She wasn't sure if they could hear her. It was hard to say it loud enough. 'You could try here instead.' She indicated a spot next to his bicep.

The male paramedic ignored her and stuck the needle in the back of Irfan's hand, a horrible thing to see.

'Got it,' he said triumphantly.

Irfan opened his eyes.

'Irfan,' said the woman. They had already asked his name. 'Irfan, do you know what happened?'

Irfan looked at her numbly.

'You took too much heroin,' the paramedic told him slowly and clearly.

Still silent, he tried to push himself up with his elbows, but he couldn't do it.

Looking round, Esther noticed that their downstairs neighbour was standing in the doorway. He was a sandal-wearing primary school teacher whom she'd always disliked. She couldn't understand why he was in their flat.

'Is everything all right?' he was saying. 'I just wanted to see if...' He cast his eyes around the room.

The male paramedic seemed to have a better grasp of the situation than Esther. He placed himself in front of him, blocking his view, and pushed him back out of the door.

Irfan tugged feebly at his wet T-shirt. A puzzled expression crossed his face. He still didn't speak.

'I don't know what happened...' said Esther to the woman. It was partly a question, partly an attempt to say that this wasn't how it seemed, they weren't what they seemed.

She shrugged. 'We were round the corner a couple of hours ago, another call. There must be a strong batch around.' There was nothing unkind in her eyes, just matter of fact.

The two of them lifted Irfan up, strapped him into a kind of fold-up chair and carried him down the stairs. He only had his socks on, no shoes. Should she bring some shoes? It seemed too strange a thing to do. They transferred Irfan onto the bed in the ambulance and put a blanket over him. Esther got in and sat down beside him. As the paramedic shut the doors behind them she saw their neighbour standing by the front door, watching. She had slipped outside the bounds of ordinary life; she was a spectacle now.

They turned the siren on again to go to hospital. She supposed this must mean it was serious. She held Irfan's hand. It was cold. She tried to rub it warm.

'You nearly died,' she scolded him.

He looked at her dully, shook his head as if he could shake off this fact like a fly.

'You did. You nearly died.' She was trying to convince herself as well as him, but it didn't seem certain that he was either dead or alive. The matter had been thrown into suspense.

In the hospital they found a bed for him straight away. Just luck, she supposed. The nurse drew the curtains around them, then brought in various bits of equipment. Somehow Irfan sprouted a drip in his hand, the other one this time, and an oxygen mask on his face. He fell asleep immediately. Esther sat watching him, trying to make him well by the force of her attention. What if she'd left it too long to call the ambulance? What if he was brain damaged? Presently she realised she was cold and uncomfortable. She hadn't had her hit before this happened. But they'd have to stop all that now. She'd have to prepare to be sick. Their heroin days were over.

After some time Irfan opened his eyes.

'Are you OK?'

He lifted up the oxygen mask to speak. 'Where am I?' His voice was a croak.

'Don't you remember? We came here in the ambulance. You OD'd.'

'No.' It seemed to be a statement of general refusal. He closed his eyes and went back to sleep.

Esther lit a cigarette and the nurse came in and told her off.

'It's explosive.' She pointed at the oxygen. She didn't seem angry, just reluctant to be blown up.

'Sorry,' said Esther, but her apology seemed futile. She was a stupid junkie now and this was doubtless how they behaved. 'How long do we have to stay?'

'A couple of hours, maybe. We're just keeping an eye on him to make sure he doesn't go back into it.'

Esther went outside for a cigarette. When she came back Irfan was awake again. He was coming back to life now.

'It's really weird,' he said. 'I haven't done that for years.'

By the time they were allowed to go it was almost midnight. Irfan padded slowly down the corridors in his socks, leaning on Esther's arm, then she phoned for a taxi. By the main doors they passed the male paramedic who'd brought them there.

He smiled at them, the first time Esther had seen him smile, and wagged a finger as he went by. 'Be more careful,' he said.

Esther almost stopped in her tracks. There was no more shocking thing he could have said in the whole, wide world. Surely he wasn't saying they were going to carry on taking drugs after this? Surely this meant they had to stop?

But of course he was right.

Sometimes, though, they did try. They knew they'd have to stop soon, if they didn't want this to become a permanent way of life. Of course it had been tempting to slip into daily use, but they couldn't let it go on forever.

They tried doing it various ways. One time they bought some methadone from Irfan's friend Otto. It wasn't too bad. They used as little of it as they could, rationing it out, just enough to take away the aches and pains, preparing to wean themselves off slowly. The hardest time was in the evenings, after work, when they usually scored, had a good, big hit together and got back into bed for a while. The evening felt strange and empty without that. But they tried to take their minds off it by cooking proper meals and it wasn't as if they'd have to stay off it forever. It was just a case of getting over their daily habits, then they'd be able to go back to their delicious weekends. Two weeks clean, Irfan reckoned, and then they'd be OK.

By the third night they were pretty pleased with themselves.

'I know what,' said Esther. 'Let's go out for a meal to celebrate how well we're doing. All this money we're saving, we can go out to that new Thai place, see what it's like.'

'Just like normal people,' grinned Irfan.

Sitting in the restaurant it was almost trippy how much like normal people they were being. Esther felt a little sore and watery in the eyes, but otherwise there was nothing to show the truth. They ordered their meals, a bottle of wine, sat there smoking as they waited for the food to come, just like the people at the other tables. It was like a game of Let's Pretend. Esther looked into the warm, dark depths of Irfan's eyes and thought again how beautiful he was.

After the meal they stepped out onto the pavement together. There was a sparkle of possibility in the warm, summer air, a peculiar extra dimension to the dark blue city night.

Esther looked at her watch. It was half past ten. 'What do you fancy doing?' She kept her voice light. She didn't want to give herself away if he wasn't thinking the same. Didn't want to be the guilty one.

He caught her eye. She tried not to smile, but the corners of his mouth were curling upwards. Simultaneously they broke into a grin.

'But where are we going to do it at this time of night?'

She shrugged and looked at the ground. 'Dunno.' She knew he knew as well as she did.

'I suppose there's probably time to get the tube there and back.' Irfan looked at his shoes.

'We shouldn't, though, really.' She was safe to examine the drawbacks now. 'I mean, it's a long way and we've both got work tomorrow.'

'Yeah, it's true.' Irfan did an impression of weighing it up. 'I know what, we could toss a coin.' He fumbled in his pocket.

'Tails we do it.' It seemed appropriate: the sinister side, left as opposed to right. They were falling back on fate now to exercise the control they no longer had, the same trick of the mind attempted by a million different addicts to a thousand different highs.

Irfan missed the catch and the coin spiralled on the pavement. Esther stepped on it.

'Heads.' Her stomach dropped as she said it. She tried to imagine the rest of the night: a quiet cup of tea at home or maybe a beer, a little television, a sensible early night. It was unbearable. It would have been so much kinder not to have known this, for the coin to have wriggled the other way.

But they were resourceful. 'We could just have one hit out of it, throw the rest away.'

She couldn't quite meet his eye. But right in step they headed for the tube.

In King's Cross they waited on the corner where the dealers usually hung out. It was Esther's job to talk to dealers: her firmness of manner made her more suited to it. Plus she was less likely to get hurt. It was Irfan's role to look out for police cars, though they both knew that in reality there was little he could do. The police spun around the dirty blocks of King's Cross so frequently and appeared so suddenly that he would have been better off deputised to keep his fingers crossed.

Two black girls, perhaps fourteen years of age, approached them to ask what they were looking for. The girls suggested that they were confused in wanting to buy heroin and that what they actually wanted was cannabis. Attempting to deploy his masculine charms, Irfan stepped forward to decline politely. But the girls were resolutely uncharmed.

'Nah, gear, that's marijuana, innit? You want some resin?' The taller of the two put her head back and looked over Irfan's shoulder at Esther.

Esther tried not to meet her stare, starting to sidle away instead. Irfan followed, also moving sideways, a smile still stuck to his face.

They pulled themselves into the shadow of a doorway a hundred yards down the street. A couple of groups of drinkers staggered by, apparently oblivious to the other kind of life being lived out around them, the flipside of the coin. A prostitute with bare legs and high heels passed on the other side of the street, looking almost too tired to walk.

A black man in an anorak strolled casually towards them.

'You doing gear?' Esther asked as he drew level.

'Uh huh.' He nodded for them to follow and headed for a dark backstreet, with Esther, then Irfan, behind him. Choosing a spot no more discreet than any other, he stopped and beckoned for Esther to give him the money.

'This better be for real,' Esther said sternly.

He returned her gaze. 'Of course.'

Holding her crumpled note in one hand, she held out her empty hand for the wrap. Fumbling, they made the exchange.

As the dealer disappeared Esther tore at the plastic with her teeth. Inside was a tight ball of expensive, scorched silver foil.

With her heart pounding, she speed-walked in the direction the so-called dealer had taken. Irfan followed twenty yards behind, his protest at the uselessness of her mission. Back on the Euston Road she spotted the man and walked up behind him.

He tried to hurry away. She followed, with Irfan following her in turn, a compromise between protest and protection, clearly unsure which was scariest: being stabbed or spending the night without drugs. The dealer turned down another side street. Esther did the same, as did Irfan, the three of them silently acting out a slow-motion pantomime for the CCTV. Not a word had been spoken between them. Another fifty yards on the dealer stopped and turned. Under the feeble street lights his anorak was worn and tattered. There were pale, pink sores on his face.

Esther spoke at last. 'I'm only going to keep following you, so you might as well sort it out.' She pursed her lips. Just because he had crack to buy she didn't see why she should suffer.

As he hesitated she was struck by their common ground. They were both out of their depth in this frightening place, both driven by their need for drugs. He was bluffing it just as much as she was.

'Fuck's sake,' he muttered. 'All right, then.'

And he led them off and introduced them to a dealer with actual heroin to sell.

Back home they rushed up the stairs, ready to vomit up their satay sauce and fall into work tired and stoned the next morning.

'Funny, isn't it?' mused Irfan as he selected a vein. 'There could be anything in this powder.'

It was dangerous behaviour and chaotic living, they both knew that. But on the plus side, at least it wasn't much like normal life.

They decided that if they weren't political activists, then at least they were bohemians. The theatre group had stopped phoning for Irfan and it had been a while since Esther had been into the office to help with the magazine. She really wanted to, but somehow something always got in the way. That or she felt too tired: it was such a strain getting up for work every day, she never seemed to have any energy left over.

'Do you realise it's over a year since you put your foot inside that office?' Lucia asked her one day, stressed and weary midway through a tough paste-up weekend.

'A year?' gasped Esther. 'It can't be.'

'Well, it is.'

'Fuck, I'm sorry, Lu. Look, I'll try and make it down tomorrow. I'd come today, but I've got to... Well, just, I'm sorry. I'll see you tomorrow.'

But the next day she overslept: she couldn't believe it was five o'clock when she woke up. She felt so sick she was barely alive. Jimmy's phone was off again and because it was Sunday it took ages to get hold of anyone else. By the time they'd scored and had their fix and nodded out and woken up, it was half past nine. She thought of phoning to see if Lucia and the others were still in the office, but it was just too embarrassing. She'd have to make it up to them another time.

But all the same their views hadn't changed, hers and Irfan's. Bohemian seemed a good word for it. They still weren't living conventional lives, weren't ready to give in to the suffocating corset of this world's possibilities, the crushing two-sided vice of working class and middle class, of losers and tainted winners. Their lives were still statements of refusal, of rebellion. There had to be another way.

It was getting frustrating, though: paradise was creeping out of reach. They rarely felt stoned anymore, except once in a while when they could afford a bit extra, or someone came through with something purer than usual, or on those rare occasions, ever fewer and further between, when they tried to kick and stayed off for a few days. The hit when they relapsed was always a good one, though now it was mixed with guilt.

Esther had good veins for a woman, but all the same they

were giving out faster than Irfan's. Even though he was a couple of years ahead of her in his mission to destroy them, he was still having luck with veins in his arms while she had set out on a vicious tour of her body. Her ankles were too bony: it was painful and difficult there. It was painful, too, in her feet and pretty much impossible: they just swelled up fat and puffy. It wasn't so sore in the backs of her knees; the veins there were just incredibly hard to find, though she did better with a nice sturdy one on the inner side of one knee. She tried the tiny thread-like veins between her fingers, but her hands swelled up like rubber gloves full of water. More and more she just used the backs of her hands. It was gruesome and difficult; knots and lumps appeared every time she missed a vein, which was often, and the scabby red track marks glared out at her when she was using the keyboard at work. There's something classic about sticking a needle in the thick, firm veins of your inner arm, but messing about with the soft, wobbly ones on her hands and ankles, where she never knew if the needle was inside it or had gone straight through the other side, was unsatisfying; it was depressing.

They'd developed that junkies' obsession with their health, too. As well as possible abscesses and mysterious maladies, they talked constantly about the state of their bowels. They were both hopelessly constipated. Having a shit had become one of the big events in their lives. It bored Esther, sometimes, just listening to herself, but she couldn't help it. It had just become very important.

And they never had sex anymore. Esther realised it one Sunday afternoon when they both woke up together, tired and unwell. She knew she needed to get up and score, but she felt so exhausted she wasn't sure she could. Tears started into her eyes. Maybe Irfan just didn't like her anymore. She rolled onto her side to hide her crying. She knew that in truth, though she loved him as much as ever, she never felt like sex these days, either. They were both just too worn out. And that made her want to cry all the more.

Irfan shuffled a little closer, fitting his knees and chest against her legs and back. A small sob shook her body.

'What's wrong?' He hugged her closer.

'Nothing. It's just, you know...I feel so fucking tired.' She tried to hold back her tears, then sobbed again.

'It doesn't help that we're sick,' he said gently. 'You'll feel better when we've scored.'

'I know, but we can't even do that.' She tried to keep her voice steady, but she wanted to wail like a baby.

They'd had to pay the phone and the electricity that week, both on threat of disconnection, and they were only managing to score day to day because Irfan took the odd twenty out of the till at the bookshop. He hated it, stealing from a black project, one that was already struggling, and Esther never asked him to, never mentioned it after the first time he told her. Sometimes he would just come home with money that had appeared from nowhere. But as he'd said, it wasn't just for him; he wanted to look after her too.

So they got up, picked their old cottons out of the bin and cooked them up into a pale, yellowish solution. Pointlessly Esther looked in the fridge, thinking about breakfast. They didn't even have any milk. It was empty except for a tub of margarine and some mango pickle.

She remembered her friend Linda, who she hadn't seen in a while.

'Hi, Linda.' Luckily she was in. 'It's Esther here. Yes, Esther. Look, I know this must sound weird...'

They didn't have the bus fare, so they walked all the way to Vauxhall, where Linda lived. Both tired and shivering, kept moving only by the force of their focus on that hit, which pulled them along like a string. They generally made these trips together, when they had to borrow money or score outside Brixton. It was part of the way they stuck together through hard times, never took it out on each other. Their troubles always brought them closer. But somehow it had come to be that the only way they could find of caring for each other was by supplying each other with smack.

Linda had chubby cheeks and a blonde-streaked bob. She gave them the money as soon as they got in the door, her forehead furrowed with concern.

'That's terrible about your work, Esther. You've been there for ages. I can't believe them messing up your wages like that.'

'I know,' said Esther, 'they're bloody useless. Always happens at the worst time, too.'

They drank down the tea she made while it was still scalding hot, made another excuse (Irfan's brother was due round, apparently) and hurried out of the door.

'We could try Jimmy again,' suggested Irfan back at the flat.

Esther shrugged. She dialled the number. She knew it off by heart.

She was surprised to hear Jimmy at all. He hadn't answered his phone for weeks.

'Uh?' His voice was muffled and thick.

'Hi, it's Esther. Just wondering if you've got anything.'

'Uh? Wassa'?'

'Wondering if you're working.'

'Umph.' And the line went dead. The nicest dealer in the world was no more. It was a terrible drug, crack.

But Ricky came through for them.

There was only one good needle left and Irfan used it first, since he'd be quickest. This was something Esther had never in her life imagined that she'd do. She'd always assumed people shared needles because in some way they didn't understand what they were doing. But now, when it came to it, when there was only one decent needle left, there was no choice at all. It wasn't even a matter of the greater efficiency of injection. It was just that a mania had possessed her brain, leaving no room for any other thought. A chase on foil would be torture, it would be so wrong, all soft and blunt and ineffectual. She needed something sharp and direct, a swift blow to the head from the inside.

But they were always careful at these times to give the needle an extra rinse.

'Pissing hell,' said Irfan. He'd messed it up. He passed the needle to Esther.

She went for the side of her knee. After a bit of poking around she got that little sip of blood in the needle and went to put the shot in, only for a shock of pain to tell her she'd missed. She tried again in another spot. But the same thing happened again, and then again, and again. What had started out as a nice, clear, golden-brown shot gradually turned black with blood. Bit by bit the needle filled up with more of it, until there was barely room to pull the plunger back. There was blood all down her leg, blood on her hands, blood on the carpet. It came to the point when she'd have to get it right or she'd pull the plunger right out and lose the lot, though the needle was so dark it was hard to see if she was getting any fresh blood back or not.

'Got it,' she declared.

But she was wrong. It hurt like fuck. Still, she couldn't stand to mess around anymore. She put the whole lot in, even though the pain burnt into her, though she wouldn't get a hit, though the side of her leg bulged out in a fat lump full of her own dead blood. There was nothing else to do.

Their lifestyle wasn't turning out the way it should. She had liked the idea of them being bohemians. It had sounded like a life that was better than the ordinary, like they'd hit on a way of doing things differently. But 'bohemian' was just a euphemism now. All it meant was drug addict.

They had thought they didn't have to do as they were told. They had thought there had to be more on offer than anyone was letting on. They had got it wrong.

On a practical level, they had simply been mistaken. Since most other information they'd ever heard about drugs had been demonstrably false, they'd thought that the horror stories about heroin's addictiveness must also be nonsense. Here Irfan was, checking it out a second time around, just to be sure. But no, he was just as much in its power as before, if not more so.

Yet it was more than that. Somewhere along the line, where once they had been atheists and sceptics, they had let heroin become their God. It was strange: they had both espoused an atheism which refuted gods of any kind. How had it happened, then, that they had let this thing become their meaning and their faith, their centre and their ruler, their answer to all things?

And what could be worse, for a pair of lapsed atheists, than for their God to betray them, to leave them orphaned and alone, cast out to wander the flat surface of this world, still longing for a heaven which had been exposed as so much cardboard?

'I can't go on like this anymore,' said Esther one day, quietly, as the police drama they were watching reached an advert break. It was pretty much a whisper, really, though she knew Irfan had heard because he took an extra-long drag on his cigarette.

The drama came back on and they watched it to the end without a word. It was the story of a couple murdered when their house was burnt down. It was their teenage foster son who'd done it.

'I'm sorry,' said Irfan at last. 'I know we've got to stop. I just don't know why we can't do it.'

Then Esther remembered: she had said this before, how she couldn't keep on this way. It must have been about a year ago; maybe this was the anniversary. She'd been convinced then that she couldn't last another week of the way they were living. It was strange how the time went by.

As they prodded around for their bedtime shots, they listened to a CD by Sunhouse, a sad loser band whom no one else cared about. The singer was singing about 'the poet of some junkie complication'. 'Feels like I'm losing my way,' he sang sorrowfully, over and over.

'Sod it,' said Esther when she'd finished, 'I'm going to have some of that valium as well.' She couldn't cope with this pathetic non-stoned state, not tonight. She took one of the ten mils.

'Chuck us one, too,' said Irfan.

Lying in bed, he gently stroked her hair away from her face. She started to feel heavy, as if she were gradually sinking underneath a weight of water.

'It'll be all right,' Irfan murmured. 'We will stop. We could do it anytime. We could start tomorrow, if you want.'

She felt like she was on the seabed now, down away from all the fuss and noise.

Irfan leaned over and kissed the bare curve of her neck.

She flinched a little. 'Don't do that.'

'Sorry, I forgot.'

Time trickled by. It was good to be so warm and heavy.

Irfan rubbed his face slowly. 'Look, Esther, I know you hate me saying this, but don't you think . . .'

'Mm?'

'Don't you think, about your dad and all. You know you don't like me kissing your neck . . .' He seemed to be struggling for the point.

'Yeah?'

'You don't like me kissing your neck, because that's what he did. And you never have sex unless you're stoned. You've always avoided it. Well, don't you think it, you know, kind of means something?'

She tried to wake herself up, but it was hard. 'Look, I know what you're saying, but it's just what I said before. He was a bit funny with me. It's not that big a deal.' She closed her eyes to try to concentrate. When she opened them again, she realised she must have drifted off. She reached and turned out the light.

'Mm, what was that?' mumbled Irfan.

'What? Oh, nothing. Just my dad.' She tried to think, but her brain was working in slow motion. 'I mean, I know you always say it and I always say the same thing. But I'm not trying to avoid it. It's just, it's not like he did anything drastic to me. And don't you think I'd know, if it had had some big effect on me? But I don't feel anything about it. Nothing at all. Not recently, anyway.'

'I dunno.' Irfan hugged her in the dark. 'I'm sure you know better than I do.'

'Yeah, I suppose so.' It was hard to tell. She'd have to think about it properly some time.

CHAPTER 7

Esther stuck out her tongue and Gudrun peered at it.

'Some improvement,' she remarked, noting the results in the form of an arcane doodle.

Esther was now having personal appointments with one of the acupuncturists at the Chinese medicine centre. Gudrun had brown hair and brownish skin, broad, hand-made shoes and the air of a seventeenth-century Puritan.

'And how long is it since you last used heroin?' Her gaze was steady and direct.

'Well, technically it's three weeks.' Esther gave a hopeful smile, flicked her eyes sideways. 'But I've only used a couple of times. It's two months since I actually kicked . . .'

Gudrun left the smile unanswered. 'Three weeks, then.'

Was there really any need to be so factual? Esther felt flustered, embarrassed. She felt she should explain.

'That's the longest I've ever managed, since the first time I took it.'

'I see,' Gudrun nodded solemnly. 'Then you're doing well.'

Now her embarrassment mushroomed. How had it happened,

to be such a sorry addict that since she'd first taken the stuff she'd never gone without it for even three weeks? What must this woman think? And what she couldn't begin to admit out loud was how hard it had been, biting down on her instincts for the three gruelling, barren weeks since her last visit to Darren's. Not taking heroin for one evening was miracle enough, never mind twenty times that, and all in a row, to boot.

Next Gudrun took her pulse, not timing it with a watch, but somehow assessing its quality.

'Also a little better,' she pronounced. 'If you can avoid using for a good stretch now, we could really begin to get some-where.' She looked at Esther earnestly.

Esther nodded and tried to smile, but the weight of Gudrun's hope was unbearable. It wouldn't have been so bad, but the fact was, she truly wanted to live up to it. It had been doing her good, coming for these appointments. The acupuncture itself seemed to help: for a couple of days afterwards she had more energy and could sleep a little better. But it was also that the prospect of accounting for herself each week for Gudrun's unflinching record provided a certain added incentive to stay clean. There was even something about her that she liked. In another world they might not have been so different, but now, as she sat before her, with her shaking hands and her excuses, she was sure that Gudrun would never think the same.

Esther lay down on the plastic-covered couch and Gudrun stuck the acupuncture needles in. She seemed to favour the most painful, bony spots, such as wrists and knees. Perhaps it was the Chinese cure for weakness of the will. Esther lay there for a while, listening to the quiet chatter outside in the main room of the centre, as the acupuncture needles did whatever it was they did.

At the end of the session, Gudrun gave her a small plastic

bottle of foul smelling Chinese herbs to take with her. At the door of the consulting room she stopped.

'You're doing well,' she said, her seriousness touched with a sudden note of warmth.

'Er, thanks,' Esther stuttered, surprised. She smiled awkwardly and tried to straighten her shoulders, tried to look worthy of Gudrun's efforts. But as she set off home she felt relieved to be out of there, to stop having to pretend to be part of that nice, nice world of hope and well-being. It was a strain having to act as though she believed she could stay clean for any length of time. And their concern with health and life was baffling. What on earth did they think she would do with those things, even supposing she could have them? It was a fluke that she'd survived this long. More than that, it was a mistake.

Gudrun was right, though: she was a little better. Slowly, reluctantly, she was coming back to life. It was all so strange and mysterious. She could hardly remember what it was like, the living world. In her long hibernation she had forgotten the most basic things. Like, how often did normal people shit? She had no idea. And her periods had returned: what a joy that was. The first one had been utter agony and had clearly called for a good, strong painkiller, something morphine-based, for instance. But she had also started to regain a little weight, filling out into something more like a living person, and she was sleeping better too, which at least lessened the likelihood of death from exhaustion.

Yet her state of mind seemed to mock her body's recovery. Two months was a long time to spend on the skewer-end of terror. Day in, day out, she was terrified. The sameness of it oppressed her. She was bored with her desperation. For God's sake, how much longer would it be? It was like running a marathon without knowing where the finishing line was. When would this emergency be over?

She was trying to bide her time, wait it out. She knew she should be rejoining the human race, stepping back on that moving track. She should be trying to find a job, but the idea terrified her. Even working out what kind of job to look for seemed like a journey to the moon. How did people manage these things? But it was wearing her down, being poor. It was physically exhausting. Her life was meant to be different now, but somehow it hadn't happened. Her giro was even more pitiful than she remembered and though she had one cheque card left which was inexplicably still working, she hardly dared use it for fear of losing it. Just once in a while she'd bring it out for a basket of food and some cigarettes. Her new life had begun, yet she was still living on weird German food from Lidl and she couldn't remember when she'd last had something new to wear. She felt frayed and dowdy and lost to humanity in that way that only poverty can achieve. While she was at home rolling cigarettes from her old dog-ends, the world was moving on without her.

She'd heard that when someone dies, the bereaved fall to cleaning shoes. She could understand it. Now to pass the time she had started painting the flat. Darren had given her some tins of paint he'd stolen a while ago when he was doing some decorating work, before they'd sacked him for being utterly useless. She'd asked him why he'd taken it, since he didn't have a home or even a room of his own to paint.

'Dunno,' he'd shrugged. 'Just seemed like a good idea at the time.'

She had started in the bedroom. She moved Irfan's belongings into the hallway and spread newspaper over the bed, since she couldn't be bothered to take the covers off. It so happened that Darren had stolen white emulsion and this seemed right: she needed something fresh and clean to cover the dirty pale green which she and Irfan had looked at for so long. They'd always planned to redecorate, but had managed not a single stroke of paint since they'd moved in. A couple of colour charts were gathering dust on the mantelpiece as proof of their intentions.

She was shocked at how dirty the walls were. There were cobwebs everywhere, splashes of tea they'd never got round to wiping off, shiny brown spots of heroin above the chest of drawers where they'd cooked up, even some darker stains that looked like blood, God knows how. And worst of all, coating everything, a layer of greasy brown dirt, mainly nicotine, she supposed, which seeped through the first coat of white as a sickly yellow presence. Year on year of junkie grime, the record of their lives. Now she wanted the place to look clean again, and new, and in particular to look different from the home she'd shared with Irfan.

As she painted, she listened to their old CDs, not the ones from better times but those they'd played when it was going wrong. *Through the Trees* by the Handsome Family, Neil Young's *Tonight's the Night*: the junkie putting on a brave face in 'Come on, Baby, Let's Go Downtown', the wail of mourning for the junkie dead in the desolate title song. The paint from the roller spattered her hands and arms and their old life filled the room like a fog. Circles of thoughts ticked round and round in her head; there was something in the repetitive nature of the painting which meant she couldn't kick her mind out of these ruts. She thought of sentences Irfan had spoken three years before. She thought endlessly about scoring. She listened to the Handsome Family's tales of death and their yearning matched her own. All these people dead and dying, she was envious.

It was funny how she'd never noticed how alone she was when she had heroin for company. Now her solitude seemed so extreme it was unnatural, an experiment on a rat to see what it could endure. The pitch of her panic rose and fell, up and down, from a low buzz to a piercing whine. And all the while she knew what would make it better. How long could she survive, stretching herself out like a piece of elastic, without the respite of heroin?

The day that Lucia called round, she'd nearly finished the second coat in the bedroom, though it was still going to need a third. She was doing the edges with a brush where the roller wouldn't reach. Her arm ached from stretching up to where the wall met the ceiling.

Lucia kissed her, as ever, on both cheeks.

'If you wanna put the kettle on,' Esther told her, 'I'm just finishing this wall.'

'OK, my dear, but we mustn't be long. Cath's expecting us at three.'

After Esther had changed and they'd drunk their coffee, they set off for Cath's house. The accumulated possessions of *What She Wants* were still in Cath's spare room, where they had been ever since the magazine had closed. Now Cath had announced that she was going abroad and had asked Esther and Lucia to help her clear them out.

As they walked up the road together, past the bunker-like brick front of the Housing Benefit Office, then a large carpet warehouse, various male passers-by surveyed Lucia's neat figure, long, glossy hair and close-fitting jacket and skirt and indicated how charmed they were by her appearance.

Lucia responded each time in a way which was graphically abusive, yet also curiously matter of fact, as if she were dishing out these insults from a sense of duty more than any real fury.

'What can I do?' she said to Esther, looking down at her shapely skirt and platform shoes with a shrug. 'I can't get used to the way women dress here. It's just so . . . understated.'

Cath took a while to get to the door.

'All right, girls!' She hugged them both warmly. 'How ya doing?' The same immense kindness as ever was in her light blue eyes and Esther realised how she'd missed her over these last, lost years.

'But how are you, my dear?' Lucia asked her. 'Are you OK? You look a little tired.' She took a step back and examined her. 'And you're thin!'

It was true. Cath looked both pale and thin. In other ways she was just the same: the same dirty-blonde hair in a messy ponytail and the same shapeless, baggy clothes, as though she were too busy with practical matters to bother with anything else. This capable air, along with her dimpled smile, had melted many a young woman's heart in Brixton over the years. But now something was different. There was a greyness to her skin, not the waxy look of a junkie but something else.

'No, I'm OK, just haven't been sleeping so well.' She forced a smile and the dimples appeared. Then she turned and led them up the stairs, though she took the steps slowly. The house was a long-term squat which Cath had somehow kept possession of while most others in the borough had been evicted. Over the years it had been home to countless different lesbians, though it was currently occupied only by Cath, her girlfriend Alice and their four cats.

Esther felt tired the moment she stepped into the room. Or, to be accurate, even more tired than usual. The three of them stood in silence, looking around at the piles of boxes, furniture and bales of unsold, yellowing magazines. A black and white cat followed them in. It sniffed around cautiously, then sneezed.

'Oof, let's have some tea first,' said Cath.

In the kitchen she made a pot of tea and opened a packet of Hobnobs. The three of them sat around the table, cradling their mugs. A cat hopped onto Esther's knee. She stroked it and it began to purr as she looked idly around at the familiar brightly painted walls, the hand-labelled jam jars of spices and on a high shelf the larger jars full of pasta and beans.

'So how's your job, Lu?' Cath inquired. 'Got the day off today?'

'It's OK, same as always.' Lucia had a ludicrously cushy job at a charity which assigned volunteers to care for the elderly. 'I phoned in sick.' She grinned. 'Well, they're a limb of the capitalist state, anyway.'

They sipped their tea. The cat nuzzled drippily at Esther's hand.

'And what's this you were telling me?' Lucia asked Cath. 'Are you really going abroad?'

'Oh, I don't know, it's no big deal. Just fancy getting away, I don't know where.'

Back in the spare room, they cast their eyes around for where to begin. Esther untied the handles of a Tesco's carrier bag. Inside was a stack of ageing newspapers.

'God, look, it's our complete set of *Outwrite*. Remember? They gave them to us when they closed down. We can't throw these away.'

'We've got quite a lot of *Spare Ribs*, too,' said Lucia, peering into a large cardboard box.

The next few boxes were full of books they'd been sent to review over the years, those that hadn't been sold off at various bookfairs and Gay Pride events. The black and white striped spines of The Women's Press featured prominently, as well as the more sober dark green of Virago.

'What are we going to do with all these?' Esther asked despondently.

Lucia shrugged. 'Recycle them? Or that second-hand book-shop on Coldharbour Lane? It would be easier if we had a car. Pity you haven't got that van anymore.' She nodded towards Cath.

Esther didn't feel strong enough for this, mentally or physically. She felt so tired she could have lain down on the floor there and then. But when she looked at Cath, she realised she looked worse. The last hint of colour had drained from her face and she was sitting numbly on an old office chair.

'God, Cath, maybe you'd better leave us to it. You look like you should lie down or something.'

'Yeah, sorry girls. I think I might have to.'

Esther and Lucia exchanged shocked glances as Cath left the room. Cath was the most dependable person in the world. She had never been known to leave a task undone while other people were still working on it.

'What d'you think is wrong with her?' asked Lucia.

'I dunno. You'd think she'd say, wouldn't you?'

They continued to poke around the room disconsolately.

'A tilting layout table, what are we supposed to do with that?' Esther gestured towards a large, white drawing-board with a movable horizontal bar across the middle. 'And a lightbox,' she exclaimed. It was making her feel nostalgic for the old days of typesetting and layout, when columns of type were cut from long, glossy galleys and pasted down onto the page. But no one used these things anymore; Apple Macs had made them redundant years ago. They'd been outdated even in the days of *What She Wants*, in the strange, hybrid method of layout they'd invented, part desktop publishing, part paste-up. 'Maybe if we put the larger things outside we can get the council to come and get them.'

'Maybe.' Lucia rolled her eyes. This was Lambeth they were talking about.

Esther sighed and sat down again. She lit a cigarette and sucked the smoke in hard. They'd gathered all these things together so carefully, all the equipment needed for a small publishing operation. 'I suppose no one's going to start it up again, the magazine? It seems such a shame for it all to go to waste . . .'

'No, I suppose they're not.' Lucia blinked heavily and wiped the corners of her eyes. She took a deep breath. 'We'd better go and buy some bin bags.'

Mainly, though, Esther just kept on painting. She finished the walls of the bedroom and this showed up the dirt and yellow of the ceiling. So she painted that as well, her skinny arms and shoulders aching from the unaccustomed strain, the paint spattering her hair and face. Sometimes she felt so tired she lay down on the sofa to sleep and would wake disoriented at odd hours of the day and night. At other times, knowing she wouldn't sleep, she carried on into the small hours. The monotonous work had taken her over. She had to get it done. She had to cover the traces of her old life, had to prove that she was someone new, no longer a junkie, that she wasn't merely left behind in the place where Irfan used to be with her.

But at night she still slept on the same side of the bed as before, leaving a person-sized space beside her. She couldn't bring herself to shift into the middle or to sprawl onto the other side, because the other side wasn't hers.

When the walls and ceiling of the bedroom were done, she looked around with relief. It had changed. But now the woodwork looked terrible, grubby and yellow and chipped. So she set to work on that too. Once the bedroom was finished, she moved Irfan's boxes back, then started on the hallway. If anything this was even dirtier than the bedroom. There were scuff marks all along the walls and it probably hadn't been painted in a decade. She began the business of rendering it a fresh, new blank.

She still had a long way to go before the whole flat was done, but she wasn't hurrying. She was trying to dispose of another block of time, hoping that something would have changed when it was gone.

When the day of her first counselling session at the drug project arrived, she set off with dread in her heart. She had already been 'assessed' and this was her first meeting with her counsellor. She waited in the drop-in room, while an Italian with dreadlocks and a pierced eyebrow made her the regulation cup of tea. She couldn't believe it had come to this.

The door of the back room opened and a big hulk of a man stepped out. His thinning steel-grey hair was cropped short and the smudged lines of prison tattoos showed on his hands beneath his lumberjack-style checked shirt. If not emotional as such, he had the blank, shocked look of someone who has just subjected themselves to a dentist of the mind. Meeting no one's eyes, he hurried through the drop-in and out through the project's sturdy door. Esther was mildly comforted. He looked no happier about this than she was.

Moments later a small, decidedly fat middle-aged woman appeared out of the same door and went about making herself a cup of tea. Then she looked around the room and since Esther was the only woman present, decided to hazard a guess.

'Esther?'

She nodded, her voice momentarily lost.

'I'm Susan.'

Esther followed her into the back room and the counsellor closed the door behind them. Inside were two identical padded chairs, such as might once have come from Ikea. She looked at the counsellor for guidance.

'Whichever one you like.'

Was this some kind of test? She was frozen in indecision. She tried to will herself to pick one, but the harder she tried to choose, the longer she seemed to stand waiting. The silence was beginning to shout. Eventually she opted for the one with its back to the window, as if this might offer her more concealment from the outside world.

The counsellor sat down opposite her and smiled encouragingly. Esther looked away. How on earth had she let herself be talked into this? She looked around the tiny room, with its peach-coloured walls and the slightly battered fake flowers in a vase on the small pine table. Next to the flowers was a box of tissues. It looked like a cliché, a joke about how a therapy room should be: blandly cheerful, as if not to upset the delicate sensibilities of the sorry souls who came here.

She glanced briefly back at the counsellor. Her face was round and red-cheeked with a crisscross of wrinkles that seemed to have been put there by years of concern for the world's troubled ways. Her straight, grey hair had been chopped off at jaw-length, apparently for the sake of convenience. She wore a tent-like shirt with a hideous pattern of random splodges and zigzags and a pair of polyester slacks. Now, Esther accepted that the pursuit of style was no measure of personal worth. Indeed, the whole concept of fashion was unarguably a trick of capitalism, if not one that she herself was immune to. It wasn't the lack of style she had a problem with. It was just that this woman clearly existed in a world which had nothing whatsoever to do with her own. It was pointless Esther being here. There was no way this grandmotherly woman could begin to understand the act of refusal which had made her a drug addict and often made her wish to remain one. It was pitiful enough to be reduced to sharing your life's secrets with a stranger, but this was even worse, because it so clearly wasn't going to work.

Somehow the counsellor caught her eye again. 'Maybe it would be best if you told me why you're here.' She had reduced her smile to a look of circumspect care.

'Well, I'm here...' And Esther wondered again why she had ever come here and certainly why she didn't get up now and leave. 'I'm here because I've been trying to stop taking drugs, but I've been having quite a bit of trouble with it.'

'Mm hmm.'

'I keep feeling all panicky and it doesn't seem to be getting any better.' Now her hopelessness was joined by shame. Panicky: how ridiculous. There were people coming to this project every day with real problems, people who were homeless, who were dying. All the terrible things that happened, the violence and deprivation that children somehow grew up through, battered, raped, neglected, and here she was, who'd had nothing but good chances in her life. A wave of self-disgust rose from her stomach. She was just a stupid smackhead, who had done this to herself for no reason at all. And now this added shame, to be using this service for herself, when other people needed it so much more.

Esther struggled to keep going. 'It just feels like there's something wrong with me.'

The counsellor nodded seriously. She watched Esther and waited, but Esther felt as though her words were scraps of paper which she was throwing against a gale of despair, and she'd used up all the words she was throwing against a gale of despair, and she'd used up all the words she could find.

'So you think that counselling might help,' the counsellor said at last.

Esther managed to haul back a few more words from oblivion. 'It's just that I've tried everything I can think of...' It was hard to find the breath to speak. That heavy, choking weight of sorrow had sprung up in her chest again. 'I suppose I'm here because I don't know what else to do.'

Although she was tired, as always, she walked home from the project. She couldn't face the noise and crush of the bus. She needed to go slowly, to let her thoughts settle. Another bag of damned herb tea was in her bag.

Suddenly there he was, in front of her, walking up the road with his back to her. He was dressed all in black, just like he often used to. The anorak was new, but there was no mistaking his slender shape and the squarish crop of his blue-black hair. Her heart pounded as if it had been turned on by a switch. How long had he been back? And why hadn't he contacted her?

She ran to catch up with him. As she drew level she went to grab his arm, but instead of Irfan's face a stranger turned and looked at her. The substitution, of this unknown face for his, was nauseating.

'Sorry,' she gasped and found herself stuck with that stale old line: 'I thought you were someone else.'

CHAPTER 8

Free the hostages of the drugs war!

The times we live in are riddled with lies. In that they are no different from any others. One of these lies, neither the greatest nor the smallest, is that Western governments are fighting a war on drugs which they intend to and can win. Year in, year out, our government announces new battle plans and proclaims a new timescale for its victory. It parades evidence of its successes in the form of polythene parcels of brown and white powder. The imminence of this victory, it claims, justifies the sacrifice of those who suffer in this war, the addicts held prisoner by the perennial failure of its campaigns.

Why, you may ask, do we make this claim, that the war on drugs is unwinnable? The answer is that the drug trade is an inherent feature of international capitalism. Any country with borders open to trade and a population who can obtain money to pay for drugs will be subject to drug trafficking. As long as inequality exists, whether global or local, those excluded from legitimate wealth will be tempted by the huge rewards of this outlaw trade. And as long as the ruling class enforces the free flow of money for its own dubious ends, so drug entrepreneurs will be able to launder their profits.

(Though why the drug trade is illegal while the arms trade is legal is a mystery to us. Both offer enormous profits; both deal in a deadly product. The only obvious difference is that the sole purpose of arms is killing, whereas drugs only sometimes kill and are generally pleasurable along the way. Could it be because arms are produced in the West, while drugs are mostly produced in the so-called Third World? But we digress.)

The only country ever to have won its war on drugs is communist China. Within ten years, from a situation in which one tenth of the population was addicted to opium, the communists wiped out drug addiction completely. But they were well organised and they didn't have the disadvantage of a commitment to free trade. In this so-called market economy, there is simply too much money to be made from selling drugs for the trade ever to be halted. Yet our capitalist politicians continue to claim otherwise.

To examine their motives, we must consider how these visionary generals direct their war. What are their tactics and where do they make their battle fronts? Simply put, the way the state fights drugs is very badly. First it sets police and customs officers to stop smuggling, an endeavour which any child knows to be like using a sieve to catch water. Then it imposes draconian penalties on small-time couriers and dealers, who are as dispensable to real drug merchants as Kleenex. Then, when these measures have failed to stem the flow of drugs, it puts drug addicts in prison, where, as we all know, they continue to take drugs. And, let's face it, who wouldn't?

Good heavens, you say, how is such incompetence possible? How can our leaders fail, year after year, to learn from their mistakes? Sadly, these are not mistakes. The truth is, the war on drugs is working very well. The poor are criminalised, resistance among the dispossessed is nullified and demons are created with which to frighten voters. And if you're lucky enough to be the US government, you can expand your policies worldwide, dealing drugs yourself (South-east Asia, Latin America) or using the excuse of drugs to attack left-wing fighters (Colombia, for a start).

And as if this weren't benefit enough, these wordy creatures known as politicians are provided with a never-ending Falklands, an endless object for fighting talk. When the victories do not come, as of course they never could, drugs Tsars are sacrificed as scapegoats while their masters continue their Churchillian declarations.

People take drugs because the world isn't good enough. Junkies are merely medicating themselves for the injuries inflicted, in their different ways, by the class system and the nuclear family. They are casualties of international capitalist patriarchy. Free trade and the money system provide them with the means to find their medicine. The state upholds this deadly political system; it therefore bears ultimate responsibility for the addicts it creates. It owes them reparation. Yet is reparation made? Far from it!

The sufferings of junkies are the state's responsibility and as such the state has no right to deny them anything. Above all, and at the very least, they should be offered heroin on prescription. (This would also make sense from the state's point of view, since it is the only way the drug trade could be undercut and is also the only way of reducing the huge bill produced by junkies' inevitable resort to crime. But the advantageous functioning of the capitalist state is not our concern.)

For those who wish to end their addiction, ready access to treatment should be available, instead of the ludicrous delays which are currently the rule. Waiting rooms should be comfortable and pleasant and appointments should never be fixed before midday.

But how cruelly the state mocks its duties. Instead of being treated with the care and solicitude they deserve, junkies are punished, held prisoner by their own need for money to buy heroin, and even by Her Majesty's Prisons themselves. Moreover, this outrage is compounded by the scandalous imposition of methadone as the only legal 'alternative' (as if!) to heroin, a substance more dangerous and more addictive than heroin itself, and not even particularly pleasant at that. (The lack of enjoyment to be obtained doubtless accounting for its legality.)

Junkies are the hostages of the so-called war on drugs. They are a measure of the failure of this discredited political system, suffering so that others may buy shiny cars and eat out a lot.

Free junkies from the misery of methadone! Free them from the stress of crime! If we can't have revolution, at least give us heroin!

'It does look good,' Esther admitted. 'I can't believe you've got Futura on here. It's such a nice typeface. You used to get it on all the old photosetters, but you hardly ever see it on Macs.'

'Pass it to me,' said Lucia. She held the leaflet at arm's length to admire it. They were in Lucia's office, where Esther had come on the pretence of being a prospective volunteer to be interviewed by Lucia. 'It's a pity Irfan never saw it finished.'

Esther shrugged. She ran her eye over it again. 'Do you think that last bit might sound kind of double-edged, though?'

'I suppose. But, you know, I like it, too. It's like it's only a . . . how is it called? Provisional demand.'

'I suppose so. It's just, it's weird. It's like we weren't writing about ourselves. Casualties of the system and all that. We thought we were talking about other people . . .'

Lucia raised her hands in a gesture of so it goes. 'But don't you feel better now you've done it? You need something like this to help you in your recovery. Part of the reason you're unhappy is because you're alone. You need to be with other people, to be connected with them, to be making something positive.'

Esther sighed. 'I know. It's just, it's hard to think about, when you feel so tired all the time...'

'But it might give you energy, to do some politics. That's why I persuade you to finish this. I know I was never a junkie, but I'll help. You could find some other ex-junkies, become organised...'

'I don't know any other ex-junkies. They're all still taking it.'

'Well, what about actual junkies, then? It's to help them, after all.'

'That's what me and Irfan were going to do. First I was going to do the layout at work. Then we were going to get a group together to distribute it, a Junkies' Action Group. Talk about an oxymoron.'

Lucia looked blank.

'A self-contradictory...'

'Oh right.'

'So first off I never got round to laying it out. Then I suppose we just forgot about it.'

'But you could still do it. You must know some people who'd be interested.'

Esther tried to think positively. 'Well, there's Darren, and Renny and Carol. But they all tend to be a bit... unreliable. It could be difficult getting them to a meeting. You know, they're busy, it's a lot to keep on top of, getting money and scoring and taking drugs...'

'Well, yes.' Lucia rubbed the back of her neck underneath her thick hair as she considered the matter. 'Obviously that's a

problem. But I still think it would be good, for all of you...'
She met Esther's gaze, then looked away. There was a pause.

Esther had drifted off somewhere. She tried to rouse herself.
'Well, we can have a think about it, see what we come up
with.' She didn't want to be unhelpful. They each knew the
outcome as well as the other, but still she appreciated Lucia's
efforts. And the leaflet looked lovely. She would take it home
and treasure it.

The tube home was busy with people leaving work early, off to
make a start on their weekends. Esther hung onto the pole as
the train swung her back and forth. She felt scruffy and
conspicuous in her frayed jacket and out-of-date trainers.

She thought about the leaflet and what Lucia had said and
she knew Lucia was right. It was no good, this isolation. For a
person to be happy, to feel that they have a place in this world,
they need to feel connected to others, to feel those invisible
links stretching out across the map lines of roads and buildings
and cities, ultimately across oceans and continents. Maybe this
leaflet wasn't the right thing, but surely she'd feel better if she
could take some kind of action together with people in the
same trouble as herself.

Yet the strange thing was that, even as she thought these
things and knew them to be true, a tiny flicker just inside her
skull began to say something different. It suggested, ever so
quietly, that for her to be as out of place in the world as she
was, on this tube train full of working people, was something
good in itself.

Climbing the stairs out of Brixton tube, the same chaos
reigned as ever. A red-faced drunk who had been there for
years was shouting just like he always did, while fitting in a
little begging on the side. The holders of the flower stall talked
loudly with the man selling socks and batteries and umbrellas.

A few people, apparently with no business interests to pursue at all, waited for friends to arrive. The racket of a Christian with a megaphone sounded from out on the street. And three Portuguese junkies, with their dark eyes and beards, stood at different points on the steps pleading for used travelcards.

Esther joined the surge of pedestrians overwhelming the cars at the crossing, then turned and headed home. It had worn her out going into town. Her body felt weak and floppy, as if there wasn't enough substance in her bones. And again something started to shift in her mind. Whereas generally she was sick of feeling so tired all the time, now it began to remind her of a different kind of tiredness, of that drug-fucked junkie hopelessness that saturates your body the day after a particularly heavy indulgence, when you feel as limp as a piece of old celery but you don't mind at all. It just reminds you of the fun you had and of how you're not going to wait for the hangover, you're just going to pulverise your body with more, because if you don't stop doing it, then you'll never get sick. It reminded her of feeling happy to be so useless in the world, because to be fit for this world's work was a waste and a crime.

At home she put on the tape of Royal Trux her friend Skinner had made her. She could equally well have chosen *Cats and Dogs* or *Thank You*, but she wanted to hear them as she first had, in all their laidback, smacked out, rock'n'roll glory. The first drawling notes of 'Back to School' were the sound of heroin itself. She thought of how it runs through your body to lay it down flat and helpless, bereft, and replete with all the happiness a person can know.

Inevitability washed over her, just the way the song said it would. Falling down was so beautiful. She picked up the phone and called Darren.

On the bus she thought of how this was wrong. This was a sin. A secret deal was hidden away in her mind, which said that she could take heroin if she truly, truly had to, if she sincerely believed that there was no other option and she'd go crazy if she didn't. This wasn't one of those times. She wasn't desperate and her drugs morality was therefore contravened. But a magic spell was upon her. God in heaven, how she loved heroin.

She called in at Darren's and together they caught the bus towards Renny and Carol's.

''Scuse me, have you got lipstick on?' a young girl enquired loudly of Darren. At the back of the bus her friends screamed with laughter.

Taking the wiser course, they got off at the next stop. Darren had had enough experience with school children to know it was best not to start anything.

They walked along in silence for a moment.

Darren coughed nervously. 'Esther?'

'Yes.'

'Do you think I should change my name to Crystal?'

'Um, I wouldn't rush into it.'

Carol opened the door to them. Correctly assessing their priorities, she skipped the chitchat. 'He's not back yet.'

They followed her into the flat and sat down on the sofa while Carol put the kettle on. A poster of Iggy Pop looked down at them from the wall. On the television, a band finished their song and the picture cut to the presenters, who took turns in talking brightly to the camera.

Faced with the imminent reality of her crime, a chill crept into Esther's stomach, but there was no way she was going home now. It was nonsense, she reminded herself, all this strait-laced living, always trying to be good. What kind of life would she have, if that was all she did? The best way to live was to do what you shouldn't. It was practically a proven law of nature.

'He left at four,' said Carol, handing them their mugs of tea. 'He was going up west, but he should have been back by now.

Useless fucker. Anyway, he shouldn't be long.' She sat down with them to wait. She was a good ten years older than the two of them and her years of drug use showed on her. While her hair and clothes were like those of any other mum in the playground, her face was old and drawn, wracked with lines and shadows.

'Hiya, Jade!' said Darren, as Carol's daughter, maybe eight years old, walked through towards the kitchen. 'Whatcha up to?'

'Homework,' she answered in a tone of doom, casting her eyes dramatically towards the ceiling. 'Spelling, it's a total nightmare, man.' She fetched herself a glass of squash, then headed back to her room. The door clicked shut behind her.

As the credits rolled for the pop programme Carol flicked around and settled on a holiday show. 'I just do it to torture myself,' she explained.

At last Renny's key sounded in the lock. 'Er, yeah, sorry.' He stumbled into the room. 'I got held up.'

'We can see that,' said Carol acidly, taking in his drooping eyelids, daffy grin and slouching shoulders with no apparent surprise.

'Esther, Daz.' He gave them each a nod. He looked exactly like he always did. He was short and very thin, and about the same age as Esther and Darren. His jeans hung off his skinny arse as if it wasn't there at all and he wore a horrible patterned jumper. His fair hair hung aimlessly around a short, round face, rendered so hollow-cheeked by his drug use that he had the look of a malnourished, rickety child. Seeing him on the street you might take him for any other hopeless, directionless junkie, taking drugs because he didn't know what else to do with himself. But you'd be wrong. Now as he reached into his carrier bag, the glint in his eye showed the truth. Drugs were his passion, his calling and his vocation. He approached them with the reverence of a priest and the unstinting rational curiosity of a great scientist. The likes of Esther and Darren he pitied as mere amateurs.

'Couldn't get any valium. Dexies and amps OK?'

'Sure, yep.' Darren and Esther both nodded. Although Renny's more refined cocktails of rohypnol and so on were appealing, Esther wasn't sorry about the valium: on a previous occasion she had seen the web of burnt veins on his arms caused by injecting these tablets. Amps and dexies would do fine.

Renny wasted no time getting down to work. He crushed up the dexies with the back of a spoon, ready to mix them with the methadone. He sucked the methadone out of the glass ampule with a long, detachable needle on a ten mil syringe, then took the plunger out and poured the powdered dexies into the back. He then replaced the plunger, swapped the elephant-sized needle for a slightly smaller one (though it still had to be larger than the neat one mils they used for smack in order for the crushed tablets to travel down it), shook it up and it was ready to go. It was a complex procedure, but Renny was the man for it. Like many male heroin users, he was gentle by nature, but it wasn't just that. It also seemed that his absolute confidence in his priestly pharmaceutical skills spared him the need for any more general machismo.

Esther, as the female guest, got to go first. Ordinarily she hated to have anyone else inject her, but Renny was one of the few people she trusted and, besides, these large needles alarmed her. He found a vein quickly in her hand.

The hit was like a surge of energy running through every part of her and up to its crowning point in her head. More raw and grainy than the almost spiritual glow of smack, yet in its own way just as good.

She sat back and closed her eyes to enjoy it. It felt corny, but she couldn't help it. The pleasure of it hummed in her head. She was travelling through a place that was dark and thrilling.

Presently she became aware of Darren standing over her, shouting. 'Esther! Esther!' For some reason he had his trousers round his ankles. 'Esther! Esther!'

For a while she couldn't be bothered to answer. It struck her as funny that he was making such a fuss.

'I'm fine,' she said slowly, at last.

'You could have bloody told us you were clean,' complained Renny, from his position bending over the back of Carol's knees, as she lay flat out on the sofa, also with her trousers down.

'Ow, for fuck's sake!' Carol cursed him as he missed a vein.

Esther just smirked. Of course she hadn't told them she was clean and she'd known Darren wouldn't have the sense to, either. They wouldn't have let her have as much if they'd known.

Once they were all done, they settled down again in front of the television. *Top of the Pops* was just ending.

At the sound of the theme music, Jade came in. 'Mum, you said you'd tell me when it was on!'

'Oh, sorry, love. I forgot,' Carol apologised, simultaneously making a grab for a needle that was lying on the table. She stuffed it behind a cushion on the chair.

'Mum, watch out!' Jade ignored the disappearing needle and looked instead at the glass of water on the arm of the chair which Carol was about to catch with her elbow.

'Oh sugar.' Stoned and slow, Carol reached around her for something to mop up the spill. Even as she was still searching, Jade was back in the room with a cloth and wiping up the puddle from the floor. Carol caught her arm, pulled her towards her and kissed her hair.

'Isn't it your bedtime now?'

'No.' Jade wriggled. 'OK, but can I read first?'

'All right, but you stay in your room. You're not to come in here again, OK?'

'OK.'

As Jade left the room, Carol pushed the door firmly shut behind her.

Esther discovered that she had hiccups. It was funny: she'd already begun to forget about these little side effects. She tried to hold her breath to make them go away, but it was hard to remember to keep it held. Also she couldn't stop scratching her nose.

'How'd it go in court?' Darren asked Renny.

'Ha, ha. Yeah, it was all right, actually. The police messed it up, fucked up their witnesses. Judge threw it out.'

'Jammy sod,' observed Carol.

Esther headed off to the bathroom to vomit. Two cups of tea poured out, followed by her lunch. That was another thing she'd forgotten: nothing made her puke like methadone amps. They generally had her vomiting for a good forty-eight hours. She rinsed out her mouth, then tried to piss but, just like the old days, she couldn't. She ran the tap for a while, but with no luck.

When she returned Carol was entertaining Darren with tales of Renny's criminal incompetence.

'And so you know how they always pull him over? Doesn't matter what he's driving, any car you like, they'll always stop him, takes them about five minutes to spot him.' She chuckled happily. 'This time he gets pulled, they search the whole car, can't find anything.'

'Because they're stupid,' interjected Renny. 'I had two Qs right there in the ashtray.'

'Can't find anything, except what they do find, plain as daylight in the glove compartment, is six different IDs. Six!'

Renny pouted and looked at his feet.

'He's only got six different kinds of ID for six different people!' Carol guffawed with hilarity and Darren and Esther joined her.

Renny tutted. 'It just seemed like a good idea, you know, to be prepared.'

'So they're doing him for that instead. He's back in court next month.' Carol continued to laugh merrily to herself, though in truth her mockery was only half-justified. Although a fresh spell of prison time always seemed imminent, Renny had in fact been a free man for years and between them, due to the single-minded dedication with which they pursued their wheeling and dealing, theft and fraud, they successfully funded a copious intake of drugs without ever resorting to actual work.

'Anyway, time for more.' Renny reached into his bag and pulled out more handfuls of fun.

Esther went out to vomit again. When she returned her shot was ready and waiting.

Despite the dexies Esther nodded out for a while. When she woke up Carol and Darren were watching some kind of thriller. A woman was being stalked through a dark office building, glass from the broken windows crunching under her feet. Renny, who'd been sitting on the floor with his back against the sofa, had slid over sideways and was lying unconscious at their feet.

'Fucking great to have a man about the house,' observed Carol with no particular humour in her voice. 'Really comes in useful.'

Somehow it got to two o'clock and it seemed stupid to go home. Esther slept on the sofa and Darren on the floor. The next morning she was dimly aware from one hour to another of Jade watching television beside them. She eventually managed to get up only because her need to puke at last became too urgent to ignore.

'Sorry,' she said to Jade when she returned, hoping in her apology to include her presence in Jade's living room, her obvious vomiting and the fact that Darren was still snoring on the floor.

Jade looked at her, her large eyes puzzled. 'For what?'

Esther watched the rest of children's TV with Jade, the manic activity washing comfortably over her. She knew the only reason she wasn't hungover was that she was still stoned. She made herself a cup of tea, then puked it up. Carol got up, then Renny, both of them looking more or less like the living dead. Esther shook Darren awake under his blanket and they all retired to Carol and Renny's room, leaving Jade with a video. Darren in a chair, the rest of them sitting on the double bed, they started all over again.

It was Sunday evening by the time Esther got home, her old debt with Renny now substantially increased. As she put her key in the lock, a memory fought to surface in her fried brain. It wasn't easy for it; her mind had been reduced to something like the aftermath of an apocalyptic blast, a barren wasteland punctuated only by fragments of strewn rubble. It wasn't a hospitable place for thoughts to be. Then she remembered: she had an appointment with Gudrun at the acupuncture centre the next day.

Gudrun smiled as Esther entered, which was unnerving in itself. She couldn't remember this happening before.

'How are you this week?' she asked her, once they were both seated. Her brown eyes were as direct as ever. In front of her on the desk was Esther's small sheaf of notes.

Esther looked at her blankly. It had been a battle to drag herself in for this midday appointment and although she was here in body, other parts, her mind, for instance, seemed to have got left behind.

'OK, um, generally.' Was there any chance she could lie to her, or would Gudrun be able to ascertain the truth from her inspection of her pulse and tongue?

Then she realised she was going to be sick again. She'd

already vomited once in the street on her way here. She didn't even have time to explain. She merely put her hand over her mouth and rushed out of the room. Pushing a couple of people out of the way, she managed to get to the toilet. A dribble of water came up, followed by bitter green bile.

Back in the consulting room Gudrun's lips had tightened by some minute degree. There was a pause during which Esther knew she should explain herself.

'You're not so well?' Gudrun asked at last.

'Er, no, I s'pose not.'

'It seems strange.' Esther could hear that Gudrun was trying to keep the disappointment from her voice. She was trying to sound professionally neutral. 'You were doing so well. Why do you think this has happened?'

Well, why indeed? There had been no great crisis; she hadn't felt bad. Yet she'd gone out and taken drugs all the same, for no good reason at all.

She looked down at the carpeted floor and shrugged stupidly. 'I don't know.'

CHAPTER 9

Esther first met Lucia when she was going out with Esther's friend Bob. Bob had told her about this stroppy, difficult woman he'd been seeing, who was always shouting at him and smashing his possessions, so she'd been amazed when she'd finally met her to encounter someone so tiny, with her narrow waist, delicate hands and feet and her neat, pretty features. She'd imagined someone twice her size.

Esther had just come from a *What She Wants* collective meeting and as Bob went to the bar, Lucia asked her about the magazine. She explained its idealistic workings, how it was run as an open collective, consisting of whoever was present at any given meeting, and had an open editorial policy, which meant that it would print without cuts or changes anything (up to a certain length) written by any woman who agreed with the magazine's founding aim, which was the overthrow of international capitalist patriarchy.

Lucia had laughed out loud. 'And there are how many people to do this overthrowing?'

Esther grinned ruefully. 'About five. Kind of on average.

Well, you've got to start somewhere...'

'No, I love it. It's excellent. I want to join you.'

And they'd toasted her membership there and then with Esther's pint and Lucia's vodka and orange.

Bob and Lucia's relationship hadn't lasted. Lucia had left him on the grounds that men were unbearable and she was going to go out with women instead, though her resolution had struck a rock almost immediately in the shape of a humorous soul called Gareth. But Lucia had started coming to *What She Wants* collective meetings and her and Esther's friendship had stuck like glue.

The magazine's office at that time was a room in a small squatted house in a quiet Brixton backstreet. It was a council property that had housed a disabled children's project until its grant had been cut. Now it was home to a New Zealander called Petra, who out of near-separatist principles had offered her spare room for the use of *What She Wants*.

Petra was a legend on the south London lesbian scene. A self-sufficient person of great if somewhat otherworldly kindness, she had turned the house into her personal art gallery. Her art had had to adapt to life in penniless circumstances, though finances alone couldn't account for its uniqueness. It consisted of pictures cut from magazines and flower catalogues and snapshots of herself and her friends, all stuck together into collages, framed with borders of cottonwool, patterned Sellotape and lines of glitter, of the kind children use on Christmas cards. Rows of it adorned the hallway and every room in the house.

The magazine's collective meetings took place on Sunday afternoons and were practical affairs, during which post was opened and its contents read out, letters answered, articles typed up on the computer and decisions taken on the magazine's content and administration. Membership of the collective altered over the years, but at the time Lucia joined, its core was Esther and Cath, with regular visits from an extravagantly dressed army major's daughter called Tommie and a passionate young couple called Hayley and Jo, who spent every meeting sitting on one another's knees, stroking each other and kissing.

The first time Lucia knocked on the door, Esther and Cath were already at work. Cath was typing up an article about a woman sound engineer while Esther opened the post.

'Those pictures...?' queried Lucia, having walked through part of the art gallery to reach the office.

'Er, yes. They're Petra's Art.' It was always referred to with capital letters.

Esther introduced Lucia to Cath, then gave her an introductory tour of the office. It didn't take long. She showed her the folder containing a beginner's guide to laying out articles on the computer and a similar one on selling advertising space, along with the promotional leaflet for potential advertisers giving wildly exaggerated accounts of the magazine's sales and influence.

'Normally we leave the advertising to Tommie. She's quite... ah ... assertive.'

'Quite barking,' contributed Cath from the corner.

'Everyone who comes regularly gets taught how to do everything that goes into making the magazine, like laying out articles, selling advertising, the admin, all of it. Just like the fact that anyone who wants to can contribute and it won't be changed or edited. Obviously that means that sometimes we print things that are rubbish. But the readers can decide what they agree with and what they don't and the point is, it's not just about the finished product, it's about how it's made, what the process is like for the people involved in creating it.'

'It's not just what you do, it's how you do it,' Lucia summarised.

'Exactly.'

Next Esther showed her a few examples of artwork from previous issues: sheets of card matted thick with glue, Tippex and pasted-down slabs of text and photocopied images, scribbled over with additions in felt-tip and biro. She gave her a brief tour of their filing system ('Post to be answered goes here. Articles to be typed in go here. Write down what post has come in in the day book.') and that was it.

'It's beautiful,' declared Lucia. 'Simple is the best. When I worked on some feminist newsletters in Italy, we always tried to make it simple. So where do I begin?'

'On the post, if you like.'

Lucia tore open an envelope. 'OK, there's someone here, Melanie, who's making a film about young lesbians. She says she wants us to write this in a small ad for her. Do we have any small ads?'

'Yeah, kind of. Put some highlighter round it and put it on the pile there.'

'All right. And Alison has sent us a press cutting.'

'Go on.'

'When a man armed with a sawn-off shotgun, knife and tear-gas canister broke into her house and began roughing up her husband and son, Hilda Hodgson, aged 60, picked up her guitar and hit him on the head with it. Then she grabbed the stunned man in a choke hold so that her family could tie him up and call the police.'

'Must have been an electric guitar,' commented Cath.

'OK, we like that, so put it in this folder here ready for paste-up.'

'And here someone called Sula has sent us a picture. It's a type of pattern.' Lucia held the wavy multi-coloured drawing at arm's length, first one way up then the other. 'A flower or something.'

'Let's see. Oh right, Sula. She sends them in pretty regularly. It's, ah, a personal kind of picture.'

Lucia looked at her blankly.

'A . . . female picture.'

'O *Madonna!*' She turned the picture on its head.

'Just put it in the illustrations file,' said Esther. 'You never know.'

The doorbell rang and Esther went to answer it. She returned, followed by a woman with wild red curly hair, high shoes and a black and white polka dot dress.

'Lucia this is Tommie. Tommie, Lucia.'

Lucia gave her her customary kiss on both cheeks. Tommie took to it well.

'Darling, I've heard about you. We're so happy you wanted to join us. We always love to have new victims.'

'All right, Tommie. How ya doing?' Cath asked.

'Oh, I'm fine. Sorry I'm late, I had to make a little detour . . .'

'Oh, you didn't? I thought you were giving it up for Lent or whatever.'

'I know, I know, but I couldn't resist just a little visit. It's not as if I hung around for long.' She turned to Lucia. 'Stalking, darling, it's so empowering. The poor bloke doesn't know what's hit him. I'm doing an article on it for the next issue.'

Esther raised an eyebrow. 'I think not.'

'We're going to discuss it,' she whispered confidentially to Lucia. Then, more loudly, 'I'll go and make tea. I brought in some Lapsang.' She trotted off up the stairs.

Esther took a turn at the computer. She transformed a word-processed article into neat columns of type, with a dramatic headline and a few bold subheadings to break it up, along the lines of 'Cleaners Fight Back' and 'Getting Informed'. Cath sorted through a file of pictures, looking for a photograph they had forgotten to return to its owner.

Hayley and Jo arrived and were also introduced to Lucia. They squeezed onto an armchair together and jointly composed a reply to a reader's letter.

'Dear Fiona,' Jo began.

'Sorry you could not read part one of 'Women Rioters through the Ages'. We will try to make the print bigger in future and promise not to write in biro anymore, except in emergencies. We enclose the copy of the *Scum Manifesto* you asked for.

'Lots of love,

'Hayley and Jo.'

They kissed each other lingeringly in recognition of a job well done.

'Shall I start typing up the mushroom factory article?' asked Esther. 'The one about the strike?'

'Ah, right.' Cath pulled a wry face. 'I've got an update. I spoke to them in the week. They brought in scabs and it was looking pretty hopeless. They've given up.'

'Oh.'

'Shame we didn't get an issue out while there was something good to say...'

'Indeed. Well, I'll write it up, then.'

Esther typed, Cath cursed as she failed to find the missing photo, Lucia answered another letter, Tommie began to compose a horoscope column and Hayley and Jo whispered and kissed.

At seven o'clock they declared the meeting closed and headed for the pub, stopping off at an Indian takeaway to buy bright pink onion bhajis to sustain them.

*

The magazine claimed to be quarterly, but this was more for the benefit of distributors and subscribers than a reflection of any observable reality. In fact its production schedule was a more naturalistic one, dependent on the energy level of the collective and the amount of material that had been amassed on the computer.

As the layout weekend approached, the office grew busier. Articles were polished off (or started, at least), illustrations collected and distributors and advertisers harassed for money to pay the print bill. Tommie got busy on the phone trying to persuade bookshops, feminist T-shirt companies and the like to take out adverts. Esther and Lucia came into the office regularly after work and Cath put in long shifts in the daytime, keeping track of a hundred on-going tasks.

Esther was working on an article about a woman who, after years of torture by her partner, had finally stabbed him to death as he threatened to rape her once again. Disallowed a claim of self-defence, she had been imprisoned for murder and a campaign was now underway for an appeal. Meanwhile Lucia invented a happier life: a character called Mad Maxine who dealt out extraordinary acts of violence to the men who crossed her. The wobbly lines of her biro sent Maxine stomping through her cartoon strip with electrified hair and legs like an elephant's.

'What's that in her hand?' asked Esther, leaning over the desk one day. 'A garden trowel?'

'No! It's a gun!'

'Hmm. Maybe you should label it . . .'

Tommie finished her horoscopes and Esther and Cath demanded to read them, rather than letting her stick them straight onto the page as she had in a previous issue.

'"Capricorn,"' Cath read out loud. '"This month you will die a horrific death. Well, what can you expect? You should have been nicer."'

'Nice try,' said Esther.

'It's fair enough,' pouted Tommie. 'He deserves it. And what about our "no editing" policy?' But Esther's look was too much for her. Muttering about cosmic justice, she set about writing a new entry.

Jointly the collective composed an article entitled 'The Politics of Nagging: Undeclared War in Heterosexual Relationships'.

'There's every reason to nag!' Esther began.

'Why stop when you're just getting into it?' Tommie urged.

Lucia illustrated it with line drawings of particularly bad-tempered women.

On the weekend itself Cath was the first to arrive, as ever. When Esther turned up around midday, a little the worse for wear after a typical Friday night, Cath had already been to the photocopy shop and back and was now typing up a late article. Esther went to check on the state of the squat's garage, which they expanded into during layout, having reclaimed it the previous year from its function as a rubbish dump and giant toilet for the neighbourhood's cats. An old ping-pong table had been set up for pasting up pages on, as had a door laid flat between two chairs. A typewriter sat in a corner for last minute article writing, while back in the office the computer would be humming around the clock. Mindful of visiting vegans, Cath had set out a Greek loaf and a tub of humous, to which Esther added biscuits and a carton of juice.

Next to arrive was Lucia, followed by Tommie, in a turquoise feather-trimmed jacket, who brought with her a lesbian skinhead called Suze.

'Nice jacket,' said Lucia.

'Second hand, darling. It's all second hand.' She addressed

the room at large: 'Suze wants to do an article about menstrual sponges.'

Esther gave Lucia a quick introduction to the gluey matter of page layout, then got started on her own piece of artwork, pasting down an article on the deaths of two hundred Thai women who had been locked in their dormitory when fire broke out at the toy factory where they worked. Below it she put a piece on the plight of Iraqi women now that Britain and the USA had broadly succeeded in their stated aim of returning their country to the Stone Age. Around them both she drew a wobbly border of black dots and triangles.

Hayley and Jo arrived and started on a joint page. Then came Victoria, a dramatically inclined black woman with a profusion of silver bangles and hair piled in a tall, wrapped sculpture on top of her head.

'Attention, please, girls,' said Victoria. 'I've found this poem in the folder.' She held the scrap of paper aloft. 'Is it going in?'

'Read it out, my dear,' said Tommie.

'The tears well up,
I'm scared to cry,
But life seems so pointless
And I'm frightened to die.
The nurse's shoes,
They squeak on the floor.
The pain in my head,
Can't take any more.
All those times I craved
To be free of him,
When life was a prison,
My life was so grim.

That scared little girl,
She got away.
Now the doors are locked
For another day.'

'Oh God,' exclaimed Lucia, 'do you get a lot of this?'
'Quite a lot, yeah,' answered Cath.
'In?' asked Esther.
There was a general shrugging and nodding around the room.
'Why not?' ruled Tommie.
Victoria went to type it up.
Having completed her first page, Cath taped it to the wall, as they did with all finished pages. The others gathered around to admire it.
'I like the background,' said Suze. 'What is it?'
'Frozen peas. I found the picture in an advert and photocopied it. Does anyone want anything from the shop? I won't be long. I've just got to go and check on Kirsty.' This was a fourteen-year-old runaway who was currently staying at her house, magnetically drawn by Cath's saintly tolerance. 'She's in a bit of a state. Yesterday she set her room on fire and the day before that she tried to sell all my CDs.'
'Bloody hell,' said Lucia.
'Well, it was OK. No one wanted them, so she dumped them in a bin and I just went and got them out again.'
As Cath left, an aspiring journalist called Frances arrived. 'Is everything all right?' she asked in a tone which suggested she'd been out of the office for a couple of hours, rather than the actual five months since her last visit.
In the kitchen Tommie griped, 'That person! She always turns up for half an afternoon at paste-up, then goes around telling the world she's a vital member of the collective.'
'Yeah, but she's got very nice handwriting,' countered

Esther. Together they carried down the coffee and tea.

Cath returned with the news that her house was intact, though the teenager had made a pass at Cath's sister. As evening arrived, Esther and Lucia made a trip to the Indian takeaway and the off licence and they all feasted on curry and lager.

'Oh shit!' cried Hayley, as she spilt *aloo gobi* on an almost finished page.

'Just wipe it off,' said Cath. 'As long as it's yellow it won't come out in the printing.'

'Well, I'm sorry, everyone,' announced Frances, draining her can, 'but I've got to go now. Hope the rest of it goes OK. I've got to review this new club. Such a pain.'

Gradually the number of finished pages taped up on the wall increased. They never worked to a fixed page plan, but as they neared their planned total they would begin to tailor the remaining pages accordingly. Hayley and Jo left to catch their last bus, then Tommie, Suze and Victoria set off together for the tube. Esther, Lucia and Cath stayed into the small hours, mesmerised by their craft.

Proudly Lucia taped another finished page to the wall. A trail of tiny bugs wound its way around a reader's poem about self-mutilation, a couple of adverts and a letter from Somalia.

'Ah, no, fuck it!' she cried, 'This advert's already been used. Look, Victoria's put it on her page, too.'

Cath inspected the duplication. 'Don't worry, we always do it.' She patted Lucia on the shoulder. 'It's getting late. We should sort it out tomorrow.'

Esther stood up and stretched, trying to undo the hunch that had set fast in her neck. They pressed lids back onto the pots of Cow Gum, then Cath drove them both home in her ancient but well-tended van.

*

The next day, arriving groggy and tired around noon, Esther was dismayed at the scene that faced her. It looked as though a group of dissolute bachelors had set up home for a week in a typesetter's workshop, which had then been abandoned, with the door open, and burgled. The garage reeked of stale beer and cigarette smoke. Half-empty takeaway trays with cigarettes stubbed out in them sat among piles of cut-up paper. On every surface were empty beer cans, dirty plates and half-drunk cups of tea. Here and there a waiting illustration or advert shone out fragile as a butterfly amid the debris. She opened the back door to let in some air and went to fetch some bin bags.

The doorbell rang and she let Lucia in.

'O *Dio*,' she cried when she saw the room. She helped Esther put some of the rubbish into bags. When they were done they sat by the door, looking out at the weed-filled backyard, smoking cigarettes and drinking coffee. A light drizzle drifted onto their faces.

'Where's Cath?' asked Lucia.

'I don't know. She's normally here by now.'

They both stared into space.

'God, I'm tired,' remarked Esther after a while.

'I know what you mean. It's a lot of work, isn't it? I mean, not just the layout, everything you have to do for a magazine.'

'Uh huh.'

'Do you think you'll always continue with it?'

'I've never thought about it.' Esther paused to consider. 'I suppose no one keeps doing the same thing forever, but I'm sure I'll keep on doing something like this. It's too important not to. I mean, what would people do if the magazine didn't exist? How would they know about the things that we cover? And that they weren't alone, that there were other people out there like them?'

'But don't you think you'll get worn out? Used up?'

Esther shrugged. 'Why would I? If I do, I'll just have a rest, a holiday or something.'

'I suppose so.' Lucia took out another Silk Cut. A tabby cat stalked through the yard and jumped over the back wall. 'It's just, you know how I love it, this magazine and all this type of action. I was working with a lot of feminist projects in my town, in Italy, and with some autonomist things, too. I've always done this since when I was young. But sometimes I feel so tired, I feel like I won't be able to continue.'

Esther considered this for a moment. 'But you always seem so full of energy, like nothing could stop you. And the way you are about blokes. I mean, er, obviously it's good to be angry... It's just, I can't imagine you not doing this.'

'I know.'

'And besides, we won't let it happen. We're a collective; we'll look after each other. There's no way we'll let this fall apart.'

'It's true, I'm sure you're right. Maybe it's just this mood I'm in. I haven't been sleeping so well. And I wish we weren't working in this garage. It's like the one we had at home.'

Esther looked at her blankly.

'The one where my brother killed himself.'

'So where is it all then, girls?' asked Cath when she arrived. 'I thought you'd have it finished by now.'

Esther spread her hands.

'Oh well, I'm sorry I'm so late. I couldn't believe it: when I got home last night Kirsty had disappeared. Izzy said not to bother, but I couldn't have lived with myself if I hadn't tried to look for her, at least. So I went and drove around a bit, but I couldn't find her anywhere. Then she turns up at five in the morning, rings the bell because she hasn't got her key. Turns out she met these bloody crackheads, says she didn't have anything, just stayed up all night talking to them...God, it's terrifying.' She slumped into a chair. 'What's a person meant to do?'

'Send her home?' suggested Esther.

Cath tutted, clearly finding the idea unthinkable. 'Anyway, we'd better get on with it.' She switched the lamp on above the page she'd left half-finished the night before.

One by one the rest of the team arrived: Tommie, her friend Suze, Hayley and Jo and Victoria. A friend of Esther's called Aysha turned up for the first time and sat in the corner typing music reviews. Once they were done, Esther gave her a quick lesson in layout and left her to create the magazine's music page.

Hayley and Jo went to work on the letters page. 'Hey, are we still using the made-up bloke letter?' asked Jo. 'Are we going to do a reply?'

'Read it out again,' commanded Esther.

'Dear *What She Wants* crew,

'I am writing to tell you how fantastic your mag is. It's a million times better than anything produced by men. I worship you and support you with every fibre of my being. The only thing that I think could possibly be improved in *What She Wants* is if you allowed contributions from supportive males like myself.

'Lots of love,

'Dave.'

'Dear Dave,' dictated Esther. 'Thank you for your letter. We value support from men...'

'...especially financial,' contributed Cath.

'But we suggest you contact the *Guardian*, the *Independent*...'

'...*Private Eye*, the *New Statesman*...' added Tommie.

136

'... the *Sun*, the *Mirror*, *NME* ...' Victoria piped up.

'... et cetera, et cetera, all of which positively discriminate towards men,' Cath finished triumphantly.

Petra, the occupier of the squat, popped her head around the door. A fuzz of brown hair formed something like a cloud around her face and a spray of freckles crossed her nose.

'Hi, everyone, just thought I'd come and check there was no slacking going on. Are you doing all right? I brought you a packet of toffees to keep you going.'

'Thanks, Petra,' called various voices around the room as Petra disappeared up the stairs.

'All right, girls,' said Tommie. 'Let me have a go on that typewriter. I'm going to write about my warts. They're getting much better, you know. If I poke around, I can hardly feel them at all now.'

'Another one done,' Cath announced, standing up and stretching. 'Who wants tea?'

'I like your cat drawings,' cooed Suze, standing close to Cath as she admired her page. 'You're such a good artist.'

Esther and Tommie exchanged glances which registered the familiarity of this scene, while Suze followed Cath towards the kitchen.

'Fucking hell!' Lucia stamped her foot. 'I had a picture of an old woman playing pool; I photocopied it at work. It was beautiful. Now it's disappeared.'

'Where did you last have it?' asked Esther.

'Here!' Lucia indicated the vague area of the ping-pong table, now piled high with gluey scraps of paper. More pieces of paper lay on the floor beneath it and on every horizontal surface in the room. Slowly they all began to lift up pages and shuffle through piles of drawings, photocopies and off-cuts.

'I think you've lost it, darling,' said Tommie after some time.

Lucia pouted sorrowfully.

'No, no, don't despair!' Victoria waved a picture in the air. 'Is this what you're looking for? It was stuck to the back of this article on lesbian sheep.'

'Bless you, my dear!'

'OK, so now I reckon you owe me one,' declared Victoria. 'Any chance of some pictures to go with this questionnaire? It's about the redistribution of wealth. Since women do two thirds of the world's work and get five per cent of the income, it says the government is having a repayment scheme and it asks readers how much money they think they should get.'

Lucia beamed. 'Well, I could draw a lot of money. Maybe even some money for them to cut out and keep?'

'Excellent. I'll show you where it's got to fit in.'

As the evening arrived, they repeated their journey to the takeaway and the off licence. Cigarette smoke hung heavy in the air. The collective hunched over their pages like watchmakers at work. Esther, Cath and Tommie took turns at the computer, styling and running out text and producing headlines in a selection of sizes and typefaces, which were handed over to anxious layout artists. At three in the morning the hardcore of the collective were still there, along with Suze, who increasingly had worked at Cath's side.

'That's it, I've done it,' declared Lucia, clicking the lid back onto a marker pen.

For a moment they all stood in the middle of the room, hypnotised by the marvel they had created, the double row of pages now taped around the walls.

Cath broke the silence. 'Come on, then.'

They peeled the pages off and laid them edge to edge down the hallway, swapping one for another until they'd achieved a satisfactory order. Then with felt-tip and Tippex they added page numbers to the corners.

*

At eight o'clock the next morning Esther and Lucia sat side by side on the tube. Esther cradled the box of artwork on her knee as they made the journey to the printer's. She felt shivery and sick from lack of sleep and she could hardly see straight, but she was exhilarated, too. Neither of them seemed able to put a sentence together, so for the most part they sat in silence.

When they stepped out of the tube at the other end it had started to drizzle again in a fine, cold mist. As the morning traffic sped past them, they walked together past blocks of flats and a string of shops, then turned into an industrial estate. Esther recognised the printer from her last visit. He counted off the pages with them, checked the banker's draft and then it was done.

On the tube they sat quietly again, now minus the box of pages.

'About yesterday,' said Lucia at length, in the privacy granted by the noise of the train. 'What I was saying.'

Esther nodded.

'You know I didn't mean it.'

Esther glanced sideways.

'About carrying on. You know I won't really stop, not like that.' She paused as they reached a station and Esther wondered whether that was all she was going to say. But as the train sped up again she continued: 'I know it seems like I'm crazy sometimes, always angry, always fighting, but it's just what I have to do. I'm not saying I'm OK inside, but I know what I have to do to keep going and this is it.'

CHAPTER 10

As she waited in the drop-in for her counselling session to begin, one of the project's workers sat down to chat to her. Esther was a familiar face there now, with her weekly visits.

'How's it going?' The worker was a young man with the eyes of someone older. He had a soft Scottish accent.

'Yeah, OK,' Esther nodded. This was a straightforward lie, but she wasn't about to tell this man the horror that was going on in her head.

'So you're finding it not too bad?'

'No, well, you know.' An involuntary shudder passed through her, jerking the mug of tea in her hand so that a little wave lapped out onto the floor. Horrified, she looked up to see whether he'd noticed. He gave no indication either way.

'Do you go to meetings at all?' he asked.

'Meetings?'

'NA meetings, Narcotics Anonymous.'

'No, I don't think it would be my cup of tea.' Embarrassed by her reference to tea, she glanced down at the mug in her hand. 'I mean, not my thing.' Though she was too polite to say so, she had heard enough about it, with its rituals and confessions, for the idea to appal her.

'Sure, fair enough.' The worker shrugged. 'It's just that a lot of people find it doesn't always feel like enough support, just having the counselling once a week or whatever. They can feel quite isolated.'

'Uh huh,' she admitted guardedly, unnerved by his intuition.

'I mean, I think it's a disgrace that there isn't more support. The government's so big on its anti-drugs thing, but then it doesn't give people half a chance. But there you are, that's the way of the world. Seems like the only people who care about drug addicts are other addicts themselves, so it's NA or nothing. It's wrong, but that's the way it is.'

'Yeah, right.' She could see his point, but desperate as she might be, there was still no way she was going to NA.

Stiff with self-consciousness, Esther sat on her plastic chair as the room continued to fill. She had no idea what was going on. Everyone else seemed to know each other. They were all saying hello and chatting and worst of all they kept hugging each other. She lit a cigarette and tried not to look uncool. Avoiding anyone's eye, she sneaked odd glances around the room, but she couldn't work these people out. They all looked so normal, it was hard to believe any of them had ever been junkies.

On the dot of half seven a man of about fifty began to speak. His clothes and haircut, like those of the others here, declared that he was part of this world, not at odds with it. He had the gruff voice of a long-term smoker. 'I'm Ray and I'm an addict,' he declared. These were the words Esther had been dreading. Thank God there was no one she knew to see her here.

Around the room various people introduced themselves in the same way, then read aloud from coloured cards. Esther had noticed these cards dotted around on some of the chairs and had avoided them when she sat down. Now she tried to take in what was being said. She managed to learn that she was an addict and would always remain so, whether or not she took drugs, and that the solution to this misfortune lay somehow in God. Altogether God seemed to feature pretty heavily. Esther was frankly shocked. Although she had heard rumours that the organisation was in some way religious, she had never expected them to be so open about it. Up until now she had innocently assumed that most people in the modern world found religion ridiculous. But maybe that was it: the punishment for having been a junkie was that you had to uphold some ludicrous belief which the rest of the world had long since abandoned. The idea wasn't funny to her. Though some people maintained that practicalities were more important than abstract beliefs, this was not a view that Esther had ever shared. Would her life be worth living if she had to lie to herself to do it? She wasn't sure.

Next Ray repeated that he was an addict and introduced the man sitting next to him as Michael.

'I'm Michael and I'm an addict.' There was a nervous catch in his voice. 'I've been clean for six years and if it hadn't been for this fellowship I don't believe I'd be here at all.' He had taken his wristwatch off and as he spoke he turned it over and over in his hands. Just above his sleeves on each wrist Esther caught the pale gleam of a thick scar. He began to tell his life story.

He had been raised in a large family with an alcoholic father who had beaten his mother, himself and his brothers and sisters as frequently and savagely as he was able. At the age of thirteen Michael had learnt that his father was illiterate. Proud of his own success at school and hating his father, he had mocked him, whereupon his father had thrown him out of the house. The only person to take him in had been a woman down the road known to one and all as Junkie Janice.

As well as food and shelter she had given him heroin and from that moment on he had taken drugs continuously for the next twenty-two years.

Esther blinked back tears, but Michael himself seemed oddly unmoved. He described his life as if it belonged to someone else.

'I won't go into detail about my using,' he told them, to Esther's disappointment. 'We've all been there. Suffice to say, when I came into this fellowship I had just done cold turkey in a prison cell for maybe the sixth or seventh time. I was all alone in this world. I hated myself, I hated my life, I was sick and tired and down on my knees. I was ready to surrender. I had heard of Narcotics Anonymous before, but this time when one of the screws told me about it, I listened.'

Then he went on to talk about his personal journey through the Twelve Steps, a matter which for the most part left Esther mystified. At Step Four there were nods of recognition around the room. It apparently involved an intensive process of self-criticism, during which you listed all your personal faults. For Michael this seemed to be the crux of the process, a moment of confession he had both craved and feared.

Finally he wound up: 'When I was using I believed that it was everyone else's fault I was an addict, but now I know differently. Now I know that no one but myself made me pick up that first drug. It's just addict thinking that made me want to blame other people. It doesn't matter what made me an addict; maybe I was born that way. But by working the programme, by keeping regular contact with my Higher Power, I know I can continue to overcome my shortcomings. I can become a productive, responsible member of society and through regular meetings and with the help of my Higher Power, I can stay clean one day at a time.' He paused. 'That's all. Thank you.'

Esther was reeling in shock now: all that suffering, did he

really believe it had been a sin? She looked around, but no one else seemed surprised. No one seemed to think anything strange had just gone on.

'I'm Ray and I'm an addict,' repeated Ray once again. 'Thank you for a really great chair and I have to say I got a lot of identification from it.' He talked about what Michael had said, then went on to talk about himself. He had been having a hard week, because he'd been arguing with his partner, and had had thoughts of using drugs. Then he declared the meeting open.

Right away a woman cried out, 'I'm Nicole and I'm an addict.' The suddenness of it made Esther jump. 'This is my third meeting today, I just keep going to all these meetings, I feel so desperate, I don't know what to do.' She clutched her head in her hands. 'I'm seven months clean and I still have lots of using thoughts, but it's not just that. It's just that I feel so lonely.' She started to cry. 'I'm going to college, but I can't seem to make any friends there. I just want to know what's wrong with me. Why haven't I got any friends?' She was wailing now and around the room people looked at the floor or stared with sudden interest into their empty cups. 'I go to college, I go to meetings every day, but then I have to go home to my flat and I'm on my own. I can't stand being so alone. I want a lover. I want someone to talk to. I can't stand feeling so crazy in my head all the time.' She pointed to her head, in case anyone had missed the point. Tears were pouring down her face. 'Why haven't I got anyone to sleep with?'

Eventually she juddered to a halt. Esther felt rubbed raw. It was almost unbearable to be exposed to so much pain. But Nicole got no answer to her questions.

Instead a man jumped in with his own declaration: 'I'm Terry and I'm an addict.' And he started to talk about his own troubles. He said he was a year and a half clean, but lately he'd been feeling low and had thought a lot about drugs. He talked about how his mother had been a prostitute and how when he was young her clients had sometimes molested him.

And so it went on. Barely would one person utter the 'thank you' which closed their account than the next would call out their name with the admission that they too were an addict. Sometimes two or three would shout out at once, only to fall silent again as one carried on and the others had to wait. It seemed there could never be enough time for the sorrows and fears, from the horrifying to the mundane, which needed to be spoken. A woman talked about the trouble she was having with an essay for college; a man described how his father had hung him from the ceiling as a child and burnt the soles of his feet with cigarettes. Most Esther took to have been heroin addicts, a fair few mentioned crack and one poor soul apologised that he'd never got into smack and sheepishly confessed that his drug of choice had been cannabis. A few referred to prison, one woman said she had been a prostitute. Most were working class, a couple sounded privileged but crazy.

Only towards the end, when their leader, Ray, declared that this was 'newcomers' time' was there a moment's silence in the room. The people who spoke now were nervous and humble, overawed by those who'd been clean for so much longer than themselves.

'I'm Jamie and I'm an addict,' said a young man in a corner. The cigarette in his hand was shaking for all to see. 'I'm only eight days clean and I've got to say, the only reason I'm here is, me and a mate both OD'd on valium and gear.' He sucked on his cigarette. 'The paramedics dragged us out of this toilet; I woke up to see them standing over me. They took me into hospital, but my mate was dead.' His voice was drying up. He coughed and tried to speak more loudly. 'Well, that's me. I mean, I'm grateful to be here and all, but I don't really know...

I mean, it's one day at a time, isn't it? That's what they say. Well, thanks, I guess that's all.'

For a moment the room was quiet. A couple of people looked at Esther but she stayed silent. She was afraid that if she spoke, she'd make herself part of it. When Ray declared the end of sharing time, she was relieved. At last she could get away from this strange place. But she was premature. First more people read from coloured cards, then Michael, who'd told his life story, handed out coloured key-rings to people who'd been clean for certain lengths of time. People accepted them with tears in their eyes. Everyone clapped. Michael hugged them, then others who seemed to know them did the same. Esther was shocked all over again, and alarmed. What if it happened to her? What if she became so sad and desperate that she was proud to carry a coloured plastic key-ring printed with the name of NA?

Just when she thought it could get no worse, Michael asked the room to join him in a prayer. Everyone around her suddenly stood up. She stood up too, afraid to draw attention to herself. The people either side of her were fumbling to take her hands. Complete strangers, touching her. The hand to her right was warm and damp, the one to her left cold and dry. Michael asked them all to start the prayer by saying 'God' and she didn't have the nerve not to do it.

'God,' she said out loud with the chorus of other voices. It was strange and powerful to say a word in time with other people. It tugged at something inside her. All together the others recited the prayer, which they knew off by heart, then they turned and hugged one another. The man with the damp hands grabbed her in a firm embrace. She froze. When he released her she rushed for the door.

A woman with a haggard, kind face stopped her. 'Hello, I'm Moira. Are you new here?'

Esther nodded.

'Would you like to take my number? In case you want to talk to someone sometime.'

The sincerity in the woman's brown eyes stopped her short. She was all shaken up. So much of her thought this meeting was nonsense. God knows, she had trouble enough, what with there being something so very wrong with her head; the last thing she needed was to be sucked into this weird world of guilt and shame and prayers and God. Surely they all had enough shame already, without nursing it stronger? Yet here was someone offering her a friendly hand. It punched her in the chest how alone she was, how desperate for someone to look after her, that this was why she'd come here.

Tears threatened to spill from her eyes. She fought to blink them back. Moira wrote her number on a scrap of paper, which Esther stuffed into her pocket before she hurried out into the dark street. Whatever was she going to do? It was so long since she'd felt part of anything. She wasn't sure she could carry on being alone. And here it was, a spark of warmth and kindness in this frightening place.

It was this or nothing and she badly needed something. What if she had got it all wrong? What if it was part of her madness, to be so unbending in her beliefs? She felt jealous of the people at the meeting for being part of it, and cut to pieces by her loneliness. The starkness of it defied her understanding: how could this be all there was?

She was on her way to the dentist's when she found a letter from her mum on the doormat. Tiny bubbles of guilt and resentment percolated through her brain, though precisely why she didn't know. Somehow this seemed to be her normal state where her mother was concerned. She opened the letter.

*

Dear Esther,

Just a quick note as usual. I had a call from your dad's sister last week, your aunt Jackie, and guess what – you have a relative living near to you. He's Jackie's son, your cousin Justin. I don't know how near to you he is, but she said he definitely lived in Brixton. Fancy that now – another member of the family in wild Brixton! So I thought you might like to call in on him sometime.

She gave the address, then chatted on about the usual stuff: Esther's grandparents' health, the dog's latest visit to the vet. She hinted that Esther might like to visit her sometime, then signed herself off. Esther stuffed the letter in her pocket. She had never understood her mother's concern with family connectedness. It seemed like some ancient dogma long separated from its practical purpose.

In the dentist's waiting room she stared around her at giant cartoons of toothbrushes and teeth, no doubt designed to teach children not to neglect their teeth as Esther had done. It wasn't as if she was even scared of dentists; she would never be so frivolous. It was just that since she'd started taking drugs she hadn't managed to get herself to the dentist even once. How did these things happen? It was mysterious all right. Now what was filling her with dread was not the pain of all the work that would have to be done, or even the damage as such that she had done to her teeth. It was more the shame of finding out just how deeply she had failed to look after herself, how very stupid she had been. Maybe it was a token for other, worse fears, those tests she wouldn't get done, but she wasn't going to think about that now.

She slipped outside for a cigarette, then put another stick of teeth-whitening chewing gum in her mouth, in the hope that it might have some healing effect on cavities. When she came back inside the receptionist called her name.

But amazingly it wasn't the horror she expected. Instead of some slick-haired sadist or doddery half-senile old man, the dentist was a small, bearded Hobbitish person, who gently inspected her teeth, soothed her fears and grandly declared, 'I treat people, not teeth!' He replaced two fillings, then returned her to the outside world.

Did this mean she might not be a stupid junkie after all? Perhaps it was too soon to decide, but all the same she felt encouraged, and proud too that she was sorting things out. Maybe she'd get a grip on her life yet.

And so, having taken this one small step, she decided there and then to try another. As a drug addict the only attention she'd paid to her family was in trying to avoid them, but maybe there was a place for her among them after all. Maybe her mother wasn't so wrong.

On her cousin's doorstep she chewed her lip and thought of running away, but she steeled herself and stayed put, though she was hoping now that he wouldn't be in. After a minute a girl with pink hair and platform trainers opened the door.

'I dunno if he's around,' she replied to Esther's enquiry. 'Hang on. Justin!' she yelled. '*Justin!*'

To Esther's disappointment, a face appeared at the top of the stairs.

'Visitor,' the girl announced, then disappeared into a downstairs room.

Justin lolloped down the stairs. Immediately Esther felt old. She supposed he was twenty or so. He had a shaggy, indie kid haircut, sloppy jeans and a T-shirt over the top of his sweatshirt with 'The Donnas' written across it. His pale face suggested he was no great fan of the outdoor life.

She stumbled through an explanation of who she was.

Justin scratched his head. 'Cor, weird,' he declared. 'My mum never said I had a cousin in London.'

'Well, I suppose she might not know. I mean, I don't see that much of my dad anymore, his side of the family...'

'Uh huh, sure.' He shrugged. There was a pause. Esther discovered they were both looking at their feet.

'Sorry...' she started to mumble, just as Justin said, 'So, er, d'you want a cup of tea or whatever?'

'Yeah, OK.' She followed him into the kitchen and waited as he put the kettle on. Looking around at grimy cupboards and sticky worktops, Esther remembered her own days of shared living. She tried not to touch anything. Following Justin out again, her shoes made clicking sounds at each step as they unstuck themselves from the lino.

In Justin's bedroom a duvet lay scrunched up on a mattress on the floor. The room was strewn with clothes, CDs, ashtrays and pizza boxes in an understandable effort to hide the landlord-issue patterned carpet. In the middle of all this was a bass guitar surrounded by a tangle of leads and effects peddles. A large poster of Justine Frishman was pinned up opposite the bed. He'd left the curtains drawn.

Esther sat down on the mattress and Justin cleared himself a space on the floor. What had started as a moment's silence stretched out longer and longer. Esther searched for something to say, but her head seemed entirely empty. She took out her packet of Royals and was almost too embarrassed to offer him one, but he took it happily enough. Still in silence, they both lit up.

'So you play bass?' she observed at last and immediately wished she hadn't. She felt more like a visiting aunt than a cousin.

'Uh, yeah. I'm in a band.'

She nodded.

After another pause he got up and put a CD on the stereo. Some unfamiliar guitar noise came out. It reminded her of music she'd used to listen to a decade before.

'So what do you, er, generally do?' Justin asked, sounding no more relaxed than Esther.

It wasn't a question she was about to answer honestly. Think about heroin, would have been the fairest response. With a bit of lying in bed crying, plus the odd trip to the dole office and the drug project.

'I, er, I used to work for a graphic design company, then I worked in a photocopy shop and now I'm, er, looking for work.' For a moment she considered her summary and was almost too depressed to speak another word, but she battled on. 'How about you?'

'Well, I think we'll probably be going full time with the band pretty soon, but, um, at the moment I'm working in this record shop in town.'

'Right.' She nodded. It could have been worse. Without thinking she got up and went to look at his CD collection. About half of it she'd never heard of. Then in the bin next to her something familiar caught her eye. It was a crumpled ball of silver foil, darkened with soot.

Her stomach flipped over inside her. Shards of familiarity and strangeness clashed against each other, but most of all there was fear.

What on earth was she meant to say? 'You're...' The sentence expired on her tongue.

'What?'

'The foil . . .' She pointed at the bin.

'Oh shit.' He looked like a schoolboy caught bunking off lessons. 'I mean, I'm not really...'

She was still standing numbly by the stereo. 'It's just, I used to take it myself.'

Relief came off him like halo. 'Oh right, cool.'

She felt pompous and old and helpless. 'It's not cool!' Though she knew as she said it that there was no way he'd believe her. She tried again: 'It was awful, a total nightmare. I've been trying to come off it and it drives you mental.'

'Oh, right.' He looked concerned, but at the same time certain that this had nothing to do with him. 'Are you OK now?'

'Yeah, kind of. But you really don't want to get into it, you know.'

'No, I know. I'm not doing it that often. Just, like, weekends and stuff.'

Her stomach sank. How could she make him understand? She could talk about money and health and all the rest, but what would that do? Everyone had heard these things, but they were too strange, too extreme, they always seemed to belong to another world. She wanted to tell him about the fear that had settled in her bones, the knowledge that it was going to kill her and she still couldn't stop, but she didn't know how to explain.

'It'll be fine,' he was saying. 'It's just a recreational thing.'

Then to her horror another thought appeared. It was awful, and yet she couldn't help but wonder: what if he had some here? How dreadful that would be, to take smack with her young cousin, not only failing to prevent it, but actually encouraging him on a slide to destruction.

So it amazed her that she still went ahead and asked. 'You haven't got any, though?'

'No, no, don't worry. There's none here. Sorry, I hope it hasn't...'

She waved his concern away.

Shaken and ashamed she set off home. The wiring of her nerves had been pulled loose. What was going on that there was so much smack around these days? It was everywhere. And to find another member of her family at it, too: were they all fucked up and doomed? Yet at the same time, a tiny hidden part of her was pleased. Pleased to find that someone in her family was like her, was of her species. It was a guilty thought. She tried to kill it off and substitute a prayer for him instead.

She was slowly getting better, though, and she couldn't deny it. She didn't exactly feel sane, but with the passage of time her body was healing. As her sleep gradually improved, so she had more energy. Her bowels were beginning to work properly again, now they were no longer blocked up like cement. Her counsellor told her she was looking better and she knew it was true. Tiny pieces of ordinary life brought her pleasure. It was a novelty to walk down the street and not feel exhausted, to get up in the morning and want breakfast. She bumped into her friend Patrick in the street and when he said, 'You look well,' she knew he meant it. It was no longer a euphemism. Sometimes whole rafts of minutes bobbed by when she didn't think about heroin.

And sometimes a new emotion possessed her. This wasn't the mad flip-flopping of emotions of the first few months but something deeper and stronger. At first she hardly knew what it was, this seething, broiling something in her head.

One day she found herself walking along wanting to smash the windscreen of every car in the street. She wanted to put bricks through strangers' windows. She wanted to pick fights with policemen, or anyone else who was holding all this in place.

It was frightening and unfamiliar. Not new, perhaps, but for the most part deeply buried. Before the smack she'd been the sensible one, calm and cerebral even when plotting worldwide revolution. And then all those years of junkie cool, in which the troublesome business of emotions is left to other people. Now the heat of her anger took her over, writhing in her head like an octopus, growing bigger all the time until she thought it would burst through her skull.

Where once what had occupied her days were plans for her own demise, now such thoughts alternated with rage. She was furious with every petty person who crossed her, the nosy neighbour, the mean-minded dole workers. She was incensed with Irfan for leaving her. How could he have done it, when he'd promised to love her forever? If she'd seen him now, words couldn't have contained the fury she felt. She'd have had to have attacked him physically, and she often came to from a daydream in which she was doing just that. And most of all, even more than with Irfan, she was furious that this was so damned hard. It was such an awful, desperate, unrelenting struggle coming off heroin and God, how she resented it. The longer it went on and the better she felt, the more she realised how bad it was. It was very, very close to being too much for her, yet there was nothing else she could do. What angered her most was that she was doing it virtually alone. Why was there no one to stand by her, to look after her? To smash up cars or put bricks through windows seemed wholly reasonable, because there was no one here to help her when she needed it so much.

Sometimes she thought about NA. They were offering support, but at such a cost. They would lure her in and make her think like them. She kept the friendly woman's number in a jar on the mantelpiece, but she never took it out.

She continued to go for counselling every week. No matter what the subject, the counsellor would always find that little chink, that twist of the knife that would get inside her. She asked Esther about her parents' divorce and Esther answered that she'd been happy because at last it would stop them arguing. By the end of the session she was confessing that deep down she'd been sure it was all her fault. The counsellor asked her why she had taken heroin and Esther said it was because it was exciting and pleasurable. Fifty minutes later the story had been flipped over like a turtle and Esther was sobbing as she stared into smack's abyss, at the black hole she'd wanted to fall into.

Each week she stumbled into the street with her eyes and nose red from crying. She hoped there was some point to this suffering, that this bad-tasting medicine would make her better soon. All this exposure to her feelings was scorching her. It was unnatural. She'd be glad when she could go back to hiding them away.

The weather got warmer and the summer sun came out. In a T-shirt one day she was idly stroking her old track marks when she found a vein she'd never used. There it was, warm and firm beneath the skin. She couldn't believe it. It was such a waste. But she took the matter no further.

On the streets she dodged people she owed money to. Turning a corner in Superdrug she ran straight into her friend Julie. Esther's basket full of nothing hit her on the knees.

'About that money...' said Julie, like someone setting foot on a rope bridge.

'I'm sorry, I'm so sorry. I haven't forgotten. I will give it back to you. I just haven't got it at the moment.'

Her cousin Justin told her of a job going at the record shop where he worked. The manager was an earnest type with receding hair and a taste for obscure surf music. With a few lies and a mention of the Trashwomen the job was hers.

She settled in easily enough. Soon she was being appalled by people's music taste as if she'd done it all her life. Whatever was the matter with them? The shop was packed with racks full of wonders from country to hip hop to Japanese noisecore, yet day after day the fools kept buying the tedious indie nonsense on the front of the NME. She tried to remember that it wasn't their fault, that the poor creatures knew no better, even that she hadn't been there herself for very long. But patience was a struggle. Customers cowered as she sneered at their purchases, but still they didn't put the damn things back on the rack. Was it unkind, she wondered once in a while? Of course it wasn't. They'd thank her in the end.

On days when she was working with Justin they entertained themselves by putting a certain selection of music on the shop stereo. From the Velvet Underground to Blur via Johnny Thunders, Morphine and the Spacemen 3, it was staggering how much music there was about heroin. If they'd set their minds to it, they could have listened to it all day with never a repetition. What was it with musicians? And how did they manage to combine taking drugs with a career in music in a way she hadn't found possible as a layout artist? The world just wasn't fair.

With her first paycheck she bought a trolleyful of food, some new lipstick and three pairs of Marks & Spencer's knickers. She was on her way back.

She was getting to like her cousin, so his continuing drug use upset her. She tried to tell him how bad it could get and how hard it was to stop. She told him how she and Irfan had both nearly died. How it had used up all their money and they'd still ended up unable to get stoned. How it had lost her her job and her lover. But it was just like throwing sand into the wind. He would simply say, 'Well, why didn't you stop then?' Or, 'But it was fun as well, wasn't it?' Or, 'But I'm not going to get addicted.' And part of her believed him. She hoped he was right. Just because she'd been the sort of pathetic character to let it take her over, it didn't mean that he would too. Some people really didn't.

'Don't you think you're doing it a bit too often, though?' she suggested as they sat in his room one afternoon.

Justin shrugged and she could tell he wasn't really listening.

Maybe her moral position was undermined by the fact that they were waiting for his dealer to arrive.

Why she was even doing it she wasn't sure. The week before she'd been congratulating herself on not having taken drugs for three whole months. It was a wonderful achievement and she knew she was right to feel proud. Then this week her head had started to go wrong again. There it was, from out of nowhere. The tube train pulled into the station and she thought how nice it would be to throw herself under it. An item on the news said a man had been decapitated in a gang war and she felt jealous. She felt that she was truly sick. She realised again that she would never get better. The idea of being clean indefinitely, of these three months stretching on forever, was suddenly appalling. She wasn't the type of person to be clean. She had to stop this lie and stop it now.

But the whole scoring thing was getting on her nerves. It was more than an hour now since Justin had phoned the guy and he'd said he'd be there in ten minutes. What was the point? Why couldn't he say, 'Pop out to the shops, put the kettle on. I'm going to go home now and smoke some crack and I'll be with you in about an hour and a half'? Why torment them with this ritualised lying?

And Justin was irritating her too, the way he kept pacing over to the window and peering through the curtains. Mainly because every time he did it, he reminded her how much she wanted to do the same. It was depressing. How many thousand times had she looked through her own curtains just as he was doing now, and how come she'd never worked out that it wouldn't bring the dealer there any sooner?

But worst of all was the excitement. She hadn't felt this excited in a long while, not since the last time she'd taken drugs, to be precise. Now, though, in a way that was new, she felt that she was standing outside herself as well; she could see it all happening. From the moment she'd decided to do it she hadn't been able to move fast enough. She'd tried to act casual on the phone to Justin, but a two year old could have spotted her breathless anticipation. Then she'd run around the flat, bumping into the furniture as she got her things together. She fumbled with her keys in the lock and dropped them on the floor. She nearly knocked over an old woman as she scooted into the street. She tripped over her laces because she'd been too rushed to do them up right. Then she muttered and fidgeted in the queue at the chemist's as she waited to buy needles.

'Blimey, are you here already?' Justin had looked stunned when he'd opened the door.

And all the time her heart was racing as if powered by some outside force. Something was controlling her and it definitely wasn't herself. It was degrading. It was only a drug, for God's sake. How exciting could that be?

She felt a little sordid shooting up in front of Justin. For someone who insisted he was too squeamish ever to use needles, he looked a little too interested. She'd been right about that unused vein, though: the needle slipped in like a knife into butter and the hit was nice, there was no denying it. But then something happened which sent a tremor through her worldview. It was a disappointment being stoned. Instead of the bliss she'd assumed was coming her way, she merely felt like her head was wrapped in a layer of fuzziness which wouldn't let her think straight.

'This gear's not the greatest, is it?' she asked Justin.

He shrugged over his foil. 'Seems fine to me.'

Could it really be that she didn't like it anymore? The idea should have been a happy one. It should have told her she was making progress, that she'd have more chance of not taking the stuff in future. But even in her padded comfort the possibility was a sharp edge she had to push away. We crave certainties in this world and one of hers was that smack was a pleasure beyond all others. An absolute, indivisible. So much had changed already. She wasn't sure she wanted to lose this as well.

She spent the rest of the day hanging out in Justin's room.

'It's going pretty well, the band and everything,' he told her. They were both lying on the floor with their heads propped up on the mattress. 'We've got a couple of gigs at these, like, real venues in Camden and we met this really cool woman. She came up to us after that gig we did and she's really into us. She runs this little label. She reckons Simon's this type of guitar genius...huh.' Somehow he managed to express both sarcasm and pride. 'And obviously Saffy's really cool.'

Esther had met Saffy, the band's singer, when she visited the shop one day. The sight of her bleach-blonde hair, tight blouse and skirt and high boots had rendered Justin speechless. How he managed to communicate with the rest of the band during practices she couldn't imagine.

Now he flopped over and shuffled on his elbows towards the roll of foil. He tore off another square and dabbed on a bit more powder. Esther decided it was time for another shot. Afterwards she realised she had nodded out for a while. Justin was lying with his head on an old pizza box.

'Yeah, so this woman,' he said after a while, 'the one with the record label, her name's Laura or Claire or something. She reckons we're going to be massive and she's going to put all her money into us. She's going to buy us some decent equipment and pay for us to go into the studio. It's gonna be really cool.' He sounded bemused but accepting. 'D'you wanna hear this song we recorded last week at Simon's?'

'OK.' Esther nodded.

He pulled out a tape from a pile of other tapes on the floor and put it on. It sounded to Esther like any number of indie bands she'd heard in her life: guitar, bass, drums, singer. She couldn't understand why people kept producing such stuff. Why didn't they want to do something different for a change? But it was competent enough for what it was.

'Yeah, that was great,' she said. 'I liked it. What's it called?'

'Saffy wrote it.' Justin blushed. 'It's called 'God's Tears in my Arm'. Cool, huh?'

Oh shit, thought Esther. They're in trouble.

In the hospital the nurse helped Cath out of the wheelchair and back into bed. Cath held on with both arms around her neck. The nurse rearranged the pillows which propped her up, then quietly closed the door behind her.

'We didn't know what you'd like,' said Esther, handing Cath a bunch of velvety Sweet Williams. 'Sorry, it seems a bit corny.' She tried to look her in the eyes, not at the shiny dome where her hair used to be. Her face was puffy and white and she looked strange without eyebrows or eyelashes. She'd been in and out for treatment after they first found out, but now she seemed to be staying here.

'Thanks,' said Cath. She tried a smile, but it was too weak to bring out her dimples. Her voice was feeble. She put the flowers next to the untouched bowl of grapes beside her.

'So, how are you?' asked Lucia brightly.

'Oh, you know, bit tired.'

'She's been in quite a lot of pain,' said Alice, Cath's girlfriend, filling in what Cath wouldn't say.

The room went quiet. Esther tried desperately to think of conversation, but all she could think was that Cath was dying. Did she know, she wondered, or had they only told Alice? Did people know it anyway, in their bones, which in Cath's case were now full of cancer?

'And how are you, Alice?' Lucia asked after a moment.

Alice shook her head, as if trying to undo the question. 'I'm fine.'

The silence was frightening.

Cath managed where the rest of them were failing. 'What have you two been up to?' She had a strange way of talking which moved only her mouth, leaving the rest of her still.

'I've got a job,' Esther began gratefully, 'in a record shop.' Then she stopped. These mundanities seemed so stupid, but she didn't know what else to do.

Cath gave a tiny nod.

'Same as usual,' said Lucia, trying to smile. 'Going to work. Looking after mad volunteers. Nothing, really.'

After a while Cath asked Alice to turn on the television and they all watched *Countdown*. Then the nurse came back to say that visiting time was over. Esther kissed Cath on the cheek and Lucia did the same.

'See you,' Esther said, then wondered if that was true.

Alice got up. 'I'll come out and have a ciggy with you.'

The smoking room seemed to have been created expressly to demonstrate just how disgusting that activity was. It had no windows, and food wrappers and empty cigarette packets were scattered among the battered plastic chairs. A couple of nurses were smoking together. Esther, Lucia and Alice sat down in the opposite corner, though the room was too small for any privacy. They all lit up.

'I can't believe she didn't tell us,' said Lucia after a minute.

Alice's eyes were tearless and wide, as if she were watching a lorry hurtling towards her. She was beautiful, as ever, with dark, polished skin and the graceful features of a statue. 'She didn't tell anyone. She didn't tell me. She just kept making up excuses for why she was so sick. I didn't know until she collapsed and we brought her into hospital.'

'God, that's terrible,' said Esther.

'I just don't understand why she didn't want treatment.' Alice's voice wavered. She changed to a whisper: 'I kept going on at her and in the end she told me: she found the lump eleven months ago.'

The nurses were still chatting.

'She was scared, I'm sure.' Lucia had lowered her voice as well. 'It's everyone's worst thing, isn't it, cancer? Maybe she thought if she just ignored it...'

'No, you don't understand. That's what I'm trying to tell you. She isn't scared.'

'But it doesn't make sense,' whispered Esther. 'She's such a sweet person...' She wasn't sure what that had to do with it, but still it made the whole thing seem more wrong.

Alice shrugged. 'I'm telling you, it's true. I've seen it in her eyes: she isn't scared.'

CHAPTER 11

'I can't keep going on like this.'

This time it was Irfan who'd said it.

'But he's on his way now.' For a moment Esther was alarmed. They'd managed a whole day with just methadone and valium, but she felt depressed and ill at ease. It was like there was nothing to look forward to ever again, like it was going to rain every day, forever. Half an hour ago they'd given in and phoned Ricky. Surely he wasn't saying now that he'd changed his mind, that he wanted to keep going?

'No, no, I don't mean that.' He sighed heavily. He sounded like the tiredest human being in the world. 'It's just the whole thing. I feel like... like a living corpse, you know? Like I'm already dead and it's just the need for smack every day that drags me out of bed and moves me around, when all I want is to lie down in peace.'

'I know,' said Esther. She tried to sound sympathetic, but she didn't want to hear about it right now. Her nerve endings were fizzing and raw. She needed him to wait until they were all smoothed down again.

But he wouldn't stop. 'I'm not sure if you do know. I know you're just as sick and tired as me, but it's also, I feel so fucking guilty. I feel terrible about never seeing my family. I miss them, you know? I'm not being funny, but it's different for you. They'd despise me if they knew I was doing this. You know, they still expect us to be different from this country, to be that little bit better.'

'Whereas my parents'd be really chuffed.' She couldn't believe he was doing it, making out he had it worse than her. And what was he trying to say: that she didn't know about these things?

The room fell quiet. A car came along the street outside. For a moment she thought it was slowing down, but then it carried on past. Another went past, then another. What was taking Ricky so long?

'I think it's this place,' he continued, relentlessly. 'This flat, Brixton, London: everything reminds me of smack. I'm sick of it. Everywhere I look, it's just smack, smack, smack, that's all it's been about here. That's why I can't stop. I just think, maybe if I was somewhere else, if I went away somewhere, I could get away from it; I'd stand more of a chance.'

Now she felt sick in her stomach. This was her home he was talking about, their home. She couldn't stop herself: 'Well, maybe I just remind you of smack as well. You might as well say it.' She knew she was crossing a line, but she felt out of control and besides, he'd been the first to break the rules.

'Well, maybe that's true.'

And so it was out. They didn't say another word after that. Ricky rang the doorbell and they cooked up and took their shots in silence. God, how she wished there was more, but at least she felt well again, like a normal human being.

Irfan put his arm around her as she sat on the sofa. 'I'm sorry.' He rested his face against her hair.

'I'm sorry too.' She sighed and closed her eyes. She wished she could undo it.

'Let's go and lie down.'

In the bedroom they half-undressed and got under the covers. They shuffled together and wrapped their arms around each other, then held each other close. Neither said a word. She could hear his heart beating and feel the softness of his breath on her face. His lips were so close that for a moment some old impulse almost made her kiss him. She wondered if he wanted sex, but thank God, of course he didn't. She loved him more than she had words to say, but it would have been such a strange thing to do now, to open herself up like that. It was so much easier without.

The next day, though, his words came back to her. It was a hard thing to forget. She couldn't help but ask: 'That thing you said yesterday, you didn't mean it, did you? That it's just about smack with us?' They were sitting in the kitchen eating spaghetti on toast.

'God, no, of course not. I'm really sorry. I was just feeling rough.'

'And you don't want to go away?'

During the pause that followed she could almost feel the blood crawling around her veins and arteries, like weary traffic on some endless American highway. It had so far to go.

His eyes looked past her. 'Well, maybe.'

Her heart stopped, then started up again. She put down her knife and fork. 'Oh right.' She said it very lightly. If he'd had enough of her, what was she going to do? Scream and cry and beg him to stay? She didn't think so. 'So where do you think you'll go?' Still just as casual.

'I was thinking maybe Italy.'

She nodded. Another country: he wanted to get away from her that badly.

'I know it sounds stupid, but someone told me once, this waitress in an Italian café, that I looked like someone from southern Italy, from Naples or whatever. I thought I could maybe go there. You know, everyone here, they always know what you are, they take one look and they think they know everything about you. Whereas if I was there, I might kind of fit in. I could learn Italian . . .'

'And you won't be a junkie any more.' She knew she sounded sarcastic, that her bitterness was showing.

He'd stopped eating too. 'I wouldn't know any dealers or other junkies.'

'But southern Italy's full of smack, you must have heard that.'

'I just know I'll feel different. We've tried to stop so many times here and it never works. It's miserable, this city; it drags me down. But if I was somewhere new . . .'

She pursed her lips. What was the point in even arguing?

'. . . And you could come with me, if you want.'

Now she sneered. A hot rush inside her made her want to tell him to go fuck himself. That if he thought she was interested in tagging along on some half-hearted invitation, dropped in after he'd already said he was going, then he was even stupider than she'd realised. But she felt humiliated enough as it was. Instead she picked up her plate and scraped the rest of her food into the bin, then walked into the living room and turned on the TV. It was amazing the things you could learn. You imagined you knew what was going on in someone's head, but you didn't, not at all.

It was under her skin now, in the air. They had let it out of the box and it was too strong for them to put back. She was nothing to him but heroin, or so this whisper said, and that was why he'd have to leave.

Sometimes they argued, in a quiet way like a headache that never quite goes, and sometimes they got stoned together and made up. He bought a second-hand travel guide to Italy and lay reading it on the sofa, while she stepped around him with a freezing politeness, spite simmering beneath the ice.

He tried it once more: 'Are you sure you don't want to come with me?'

She couldn't even speak. She just shook her head. She couldn't do it, trail along after someone who didn't want her. Besides, another fear had awoken now, coiling like something cold in her belly. At first she'd wanted to laugh in his face: you're kidding yourself, you won't get clean, being somewhere different won't change anything at all. It's you, it's inside you, it's not this city that makes you take drugs. But then the doubt had come. What if he was really going to do it? What if he was really going to stop and she couldn't? All this time, without ever thinking about it, it had been part of their landscape that he was the worse junkie because he'd started first. He'd introduced her to it and he'd taken it for longer. Now without that certainty she was lost and falling, her bones melting inside her, ashamed, helpless, invertebrate, ex-human.

He phoned his parents for the money, the first time he'd ever borrowed from them, and bought a coach ticket for Rome. He went to the doctor and got methadone to see him through the journey and help him wean himself off gently when he got there. She wouldn't watch him pack. She went to visit Darren and didn't come back until the next day, just before he was due to leave.

After he'd gone she tried not to look around her, tried to run along on her rails, working, scoring, moving from one room to another to shoot up, eat, sleep. Once in a while one of the dealers who knew them best, Ricky or Mark or Jay, would ask after him: 'Irfan all right? Haven't seen him in a while.'

She found she couldn't say it. 'Yeah, he's OK,' was all that would pass through her lips.

And after a while they stopped asking.

But if she forgot to keep her eyes straight ahead and so much as glanced around her, there he was. It was like living with a ghost. He seemed to take up more space in the flat than she did, all those things she couldn't bear to touch: the Rizlas on the table, the Coke in the fridge, an old razor in the bathroom, a jacket in the hall, books, boxes, clothes, letters, stray hairs, words, their life together gone, his key in the door coming back.

She had her armour, though, against this sorrow and she did her best with it. Every now and then she caught a whisper of what heroin used to do for her. Because when it's good and new and you haven't been working away at it for years, in its warmth and peace and safety it feels like love.

CHAPTER 12

What a dirty, disgusting, low-down liar she was. She stumbled out of her counselling session sick with shame. On the street she couldn't look anyone in the eye. She wanted to be invisible, to crawl away and die like the sick creature that she was. How could she have said a thing like that about her dad?

The counsellor had tried it before, but Esther had been firm: you couldn't go making a big deal out of such trivial bits of nothing. But this time she'd cornered her with a crafty manoeuvre. She'd asked her, 'Do you trust your dad?'

And everything had fallen to bits.

It was like falling down a hole. You were walking along, the ground level and solid beneath your feet, and you never imagined it could be otherwise. Then you took a step which seemed like any other and suddenly you were falling, down into this darkness, into another world.

But it couldn't be true. Her dad was a decent person. He'd been good to them. And he'd had it hard. Her mum had seemed to flourish after they'd split up: Esther had been proud to watch her, her confidence coming back, extending cautious feelers into the world. But by the same measure her dad had grown smaller. There he was in that flat, the ironing board in one corner, making fish fingers and oven chips for her and Dominic when they visited, the three of them squashed around the little kitchen table. She'd felt so sorry for him and a little guilty too, because secretly she'd been happy that the trouble was over and her parents were apart.

She couldn't put the dad she knew and this thing she was saying together. It would make her head explode.

Now there was nowhere safe. On the street her body seemed to scream like a siren: that anyone could touch her, she wouldn't be able to stop them. Back at the flat she double-locked the door, but there was no respite because this thing she was saying, this lie, was inside her, it was with her all the time. She wanted to climb into bed, like she always did when things were too much, but she couldn't because beds were for sex. Under the covers there'd be her body, shameful and dirty, reminding her of how she'd made this thing happen. Her head was ringing with fear, so loud she couldn't think. Even on this warm day she was shivering. She lay down on the sofa with her coat over her and cried, doubled up and nauseous from the sobbing, hating herself as she did it, a nasty piece of work like her feeling sorry for herself.

The next day she woke up with a weight of dread inside her. Something terrible had happened and any second she'd remember what it was. Sure enough a moment later there it was: the monster she'd released with a few words on an ordinary Tuesday morning. This earthquake that had shaken everything apart.

Gingerly she got out of bed and, moving as carefully as she could, got ready for work. There was a certain numbness in her that she was reluctant to disturb.

The world outside was wide, bright and strange. Strange because it looked so much like the old one, before this happened, which was ludicrous because it was now completely different. This thing that she'd discovered pressed in on her as she walked, making it hard to move naturally. Everything seemed dangerous.

At work she said hello to the others and tried to put up a screen which they wouldn't see through, but it was difficult because words seemed to be in short supply. She could only give up a bare minimum. Her face felt stiff and expressionless. She delivered herself gladly into the distraction of work. Her living self had withdrawn to some hidden place inside and left a robot imitation to serve customers.

Gradually, though, the familiar activity began to thaw her. The manager, Nick, came out to serve with her for a while and at first she was faking it as they chatted, but slowly she was drawn more genuinely into the conversation. A beggar with a flushed, alcoholic face stumbled into the shop stinking powerfully of piss and together they guided him out again. She was beginning to do quite well at not thinking. The next time it came back to her, the balance had shifted, so that it seemed less overwhelming, less real in comparison to the life she was living here and now, the life she was used to.

She didn't want to be alone that evening, so she went up to see Lucia and, although they talked for hours, she never got round to mentioning this thing that had tried to tip her world onto a different axis. The next morning she wasn't so scared when she woke up. Nervous, yes, but then the expected blow didn't come. It began to occur to her that she'd been getting it all out of proportion. She must have given the counsellor the wrong idea, exaggerated it somehow. It was madness to say that it was such a big deal. Surely plenty of fathers behaved that way around their daughters. It was entirely banal.

At the shop they offered her extra work on the day of her next counselling session and she decided to take it. God knows, she needed the money. She would have to tell the counsellor that between them they'd made a mistake, that whatever it was that was wrong with her, it couldn't be this. But she was in no great rush to see her again. She was feeling better now and she didn't exactly mind the idea of missing out on a week's brain surgery.

On days when she was working with Justin, he told her about the band's progress. He arrived one morning with the news that the woman with the record label, Lesley, it turned out her name was, had booked studio time for the band to record an album. Joyful as he was, the concept clearly made no sense to him. He announced it in the tone of, yeah, I've been selected to be the first bass player on Mars, take-off's next Thursday.

'And she's giving us money for instruments.' He lowered his voice, his grin stretching ear to ear. 'She's giving me two hundred quid tonight. Cash. I'm going into town on my day off, gonna go up Charing Cross Road, get myself a decent bass, not that piece of rubbish I've been playing.' A flick of the hand dismissed his old guitar to an imaginary skip.

A teenager came to the counter with the new Stereophonics album in his hand. Esther looked at him pityingly. Justin put The Strands on the stereo. The song was 'X Hits the Spot'.

'Well, just you make sure all that money goes on the guitar,' she warned him mock-sternly. As soon as she'd said it, she felt guilty. It wasn't a joke, this drug. She shouldn't be encouraging him.

The day after that he was late in. Hurrying into the back to take his coat off, he avoided Esther's eye. Most of the morning he wasn't working with her. He was downstairs in the basement with the country 'n' western, jazz and world music.

A subsonic thought was worrying at her consciousness, but she couldn't get hold of it. Then, after he'd been sent back upstairs to work with Esther, he rang up three purchases wrong, turned a funny shade of white and ran to the toilet with his hand over his mouth.

'You fucker,' she scolded when he got back, 'you're stoned.'

'No,' he smirked, his pale irises strangely bright around the tiny specks of his pupils.

Esther discovered she no longer wanted to be standing next to him. On the one hand she suspected that something very bad was going on, but on the other it was disconcerting how appealing it still looked. She went off to tidy the American punk/hardcore section.

A few days later when he came in after his day off she remembered. 'Did you get it, then?'

'What?' He looked shifty.

She spread her hands. 'Your new bass, of course.'

'Uh huh,' he giggled nervously. 'I was, like, going to, but there was this kind of technical problem. I, uh, borrowed a bit of that money and I thought I'd better not get it until I had the two hundred again. Otherwise she might get suspicious, if I only got a cheap one...' He sneaked a glance at her, then went back to looking at his shoes. He seemed both embarrassed and incredibly pleased with himself.

She served the next customer with two tickets for Skunk Anansie. When she looked round Justin was still upright behind the counter, but his eyes were closed and his head was starting to fall forwards. She nudged him hard.

'For fuck's sake!'

'Oh yeah, sorry.' He snapped upright, feigning alertness.

'You've got to stop this. I'm serious. No, really. You don't know what you're getting into. You're going to get in such a mess.'

He smiled nervously. His hand went up unthinkingly to rub his nose. 'Yeah, I will, honestly. I mean, I'm not going to do it at all next week. That's when we're going into the studio. I've taken the week off and obviously we've got to be quite... together.'

A new thought occurred to her. 'The rest of the band, they're not all...'

'No... at least, Stanton isn't.' This was their drummer. 'Except for just a tiny bit...'

Esther opened her mouth to say something, then realised she'd said it all already. What could she tell him that would make a difference? She'd better think of it soon, that was for sure.

The day of her next counselling session something strange happened. She hadn't slept that late in ages. However unwillingly, she was usually still springing awake bright and early, as she had done ever since she'd kicked. Yet on this particular Tuesday she stayed sound asleep until after eleven, which was when the session was due to start. She stumbled groggily to the phone and called the counsellor to apologise.

'I see,' she said drily. 'And do you think you'll be able to get here next week?'

'Of course.' That was the trouble with counsellors. They could never accept that a mistake was simply a mistake, that there wasn't some subconscious motive at work. 'I just overslept.'

'All right, but please try to make it. There are plenty of other people who want counselling too.'

Esther hung up, duly chastised.

'I just don't know what we're going to do.' As they sat in the shop's small office, Justin stared dejectedly into his mug of tea.

Esther had missed him during his week off. There was no amusement value in playing songs about heroin by herself.

'You don't realise how expensive studio time is. We didn't, I mean. I think it might have been better if she'd booked our days to start in the afternoon, or maybe even the evening. Do you think you can do that?'

'I'm not sure.'

'I mean, I got there quite early a couple of times. Saffy was definitely the worst.' He sighed. 'I dunno. We've got to make it up to Lesley somehow. It'd be really awful if the label closed down. Maybe we could do some benefit gigs and raise some money for her. But then, not that many people come to our gigs...' He rubbed his forehead. 'It just wasn't a good idea, though, was it? Putting all her money into one band?'

'Well, with hindsight, no...'

But Esther didn't try to lecture him anymore. She'd remembered something she'd once heard: that you can never stop anyone taking drugs; you can only try to help them once they've made the decision themselves. The relief this had brought her was immense. She would help him, if she could, when the time came. Meanwhile she had to let him go his own way.

Back with her counsellor she explained the problem, that they'd got it all wrong, this business with her dad.

The expression on her kindly, serious face made Esther want to spit. The counsellor had been expecting this. She reckoned she knew it all so well that she could guess exactly what Esther was going to turn up and say.

'So you felt safe around your father?'

It was the same question again. How easily she did it, knocked down all her defences like a stack of toy bricks. After a moment Esther realised she was holding her breath. She released it slowly. She looked around her, wondering if there were really no get-out, but it seemed not. At last she answered: 'No.' And she was falling down that hole again.

She had slipped through a sliding door into a double reality. It was like a split screen in a film. Half of her believed her dad had done something wrong to her, this thing her counsellor called abuse, the other knew it couldn't be true because her dad wouldn't do that. One half said she was an ungrateful, spiteful, dirty-minded liar. The other said, look at the damage, the mess your life has been. Did you do this to yourself for no reason? But that was worse, even worse than being a filthy liar. She could hardly bear to touch herself, to wash herself in the bath, because of this thing she was threatening to become: a victim.

She stumbled into work and stumbled through the day, the panic screaming through her body, an electrical storm whirling between the split halves of reality. An abyss was waiting right beside her. If it pulled her in, the whole story of her life would be changed; she'd be a different person, taken over by this fact. A victim. A statistic. A tragic story. She couldn't bear it. If she let this thing be true, that's what she'd be and what could be worse than that, to have her individuality, her control all gone, to be nothing but a victim?

She called Lucia and even as she told her, she despised herself. To be making such a fuss, when other people coped with so much worse.

'But he was sleazy with you?' Lucia asked.

'Yeah.'

'Like how?'

She could hardly say it. 'Just kind of a bit off colour, stuff he said, the way he touched me . . .' The words were foul in her mouth. Now Lucia would know how disgusting she was. Her own father.

'So you were frightened?'

'I suppose...'

'And ashamed?'

Esther tried to say yes, but she was choking on it. Tears poured silently down her face. She was sitting on the floor, the phone to her ear, her knees pulled up tight against her chest. It sounded so plausible, what Lucia was saying. In a way she could see the sense of it. But the problem was that Lucia didn't know. She was only saying these things because she was her friend. Anyone else would hate her.

It was so strange how it had changed. It wasn't even new, this stuff that Esther was saying. She'd known for years how he'd been with her, ever since she'd first remembered. And maybe the shape of it had always been known to her, the silhouette, perhaps, if not the solid mass of it, the dark outline described by her denial. How weird then that it could make so much difference, to say that it wasn't nothing, it was something. All this horror just because someone had made her say it mattered.

She was scared of Justin. She couldn't go near his house, or Darren's. There was nothing in the world she wanted more than heroin.

Could people see that she was insane? Justin, the other people at work? Because that's what you were, if you believed two opposite things at once.

She didn't know how to do anything anymore, because everything had got so different. She was faking it, pretending, copying the things she used to do. She served customers, checked the stock, went to the bank for change and all the time she was covering up, hiding the fact that she'd gone mad.

Her mum phoned, her regular call. She gave Esther the usual family reports: her brother's trouble at work, her grandfather's operation.

'Any news from your end?' her mother asked.

Esther shrugged and shook her head to make her words sound more convincing. 'No, not really. Just trogging along, the usual stuff.'

She searched for something more to say, some cheery snippet, but there was nothing there. The pause scared her. Her mum mustn't guess there was anything wrong. She'd been lying to her for years, of course. Whether she'd been aware of her drug use, she didn't know, but she'd always done her best to conceal it. Sometimes lately she'd wanted to let her know that things were getting better, but it was hard. There was no point worrying her with troubles that were past and gone. Now, though, her efforts at deception were redoubled. She had to get it right. If she had ever hidden anything, she must hide this now.

Her mother's voice cut into her thoughts. 'All right then. Well, I'll probably speak to you next week.'

For a millisecond Esther was surprised it had been so easy, but the thought died almost before it was born. If she hadn't been trying so hard, she might have wondered at how peculiarly satisfied her mother had always been with her excuses, what a curious lack of curiosity she showed. But she had no time to think about that now. The matter in hand was too important. If there was one thing in this world her mum must never know, it was this. It would break her heart.

Day by day she was swimming through this surging, stormy water. It was exhausting. And the seabed was always there beneath her, inviting. She was an alien from another galaxy, a camel in the jungle: the world had become that strange to her, that difficult.

Her very body was wrong. She didn't want it anymore; its presence appalled her. She could hardly function, trapped inside this thing. She didn't want to have breasts, a female shape, a cunt. She wanted to be abstract, to be nothing but mind. She'd always had that inclination, but now her hatred of the physical had become desperate. It wasn't safe to have a body, because it meant that people could get to you. They could degrade you, humiliate you.

Only now she was so crazy that her mind was no safe place either. There was nowhere to go. Except, of course, for that one escape she knew so well, and God, how she wanted it.

All day long her mind was rattling back and forth. He couldn't have done it. She kept getting stuck on that. That was why it was impossible. The dad she knew couldn't have held that thought in his mind. It defeated her understanding. What did you think about when you acted that way?

CHAPTER 13

After Irfan had gone she did try to stop once. She got in all the pills and a bottle of multivitamins and tried to tell herself it would be easier now she was on her own, no couple thing to drag her down. She tore up all her dealers' numbers, took her last, hefty shot and prepared to get sick.

The next day the size of that farewell left her in a thick, heavy sleep until six. She awoke sick and shaking, as she always did when she slept late. The moment she saw it was dark outside, she panicked. What if it was too late to get hold of anyone?

Then she remembered: of course, it was over. There was no phonecall to be made. Finished, ended, no more.

She knew the truth straight away; it wasn't even a matter of arguing it through: she had simply been lying to herself. She wasn't going to stop. Surely she would sometime, but that time wasn't now. She didn't know why she'd even pretended.

She went to the bin where she'd thrown the torn up bits of paper and their biro'd numbers. It was easy enough to spot the pieces of the yellow Post-it note which had had Jay's number on it. The rest she'd get back from other people. As quickly as she could she fitted the yellow scraps together until a final corner completed the number. Trying not to think at all, she picked up the receiver and dialled.

It was naked now. There was nothing to hide behind anymore. She wasn't doing it because it was part of her life with Irfan. She wasn't doing it because he was worse than her and he was stopping her from giving up. She was doing it because she was a junkie. She was utterly addicted and her life was going down the toilet and there was nothing she could do to stop it.

She felt like something you might find down a drain.

She was all alone, a cell in that fluid and single-minded organism that is the community of junkies, in which it is understood that heroin comes before all else. Sometimes Lucia phoned her, but she rarely returned her calls and when Lucia visited it always seemed to be at the wrong time. She was either asleep or fidgeting for her next shot and either way she just wanted her to go away. She spent more time with her dealers than with her supposed friend.

She hated her downstairs neighbour and he hated her. When he passed her coming in or out he would stare at her as he said a curt hello, scanning for signs of her crime. Jay told her one day that whenever he rang her doorbell, seconds later the neighbour's face would come poking around his net curtain. So the next evening when Jay made his regular visit, she stepped outside the front door and waved hello just as his face appeared. The net curtain flicked furiously shut.

Darren would come to stay with her for days at a time. Sometimes, when the waiting was over and the dealer had been and gone, when they were sitting comfortably with the TV on, he would ask her, 'Have you heard from Irfan, then?'

She always shook her head.

Darren seemed depressed and often she meant to ask him how he was. Maybe he meant to ask her the same, but when they were nodding out in front of the TV together, conversations drifted and stretched over hours, falling into holes in space along the way. Time slipped by and questions were always postponed. They couldn't help each other.

Where once she had been pursuing smack's imitation of love, now love was no longer in it. What she was looking for now was something darker and far older.

One day at work her boss tapped her on the shoulder. She came to with a jolt. On her screen was the layout for an advert, a woman's face smiling joyfully beside the text. What on earth was she meant to be doing with it?

'Esther,' her boss said quietly, 'can I have a word?'

As she followed him through the tall, white-painted office with its high, arched windows and network of computers, she tried to think of excuses for whatever misdemeanour might have been noticed. But the list of possible crimes was so long, it put her head in a spin.

Her boss sat down behind his desk and gestured for her to sit opposite. He looked a little tired today, with creases settled in behind his designer glasses, but he was still as neat as ever. She didn't know how he managed it. Even that little covering of beard, always the same length, it had to be so much effort.

'Esther, I'm really sorry, but this isn't working out, is it? I know you've been with us a long time, but I think it would be better all round if we called it a day.'

She waited, but it seemed he was leaving it short.

'Oh right.' She couldn't see any point in arguing: it would only get humiliating. The only surprise was that it hadn't happened sooner. Without meeting his eye, she stood up and went to the door, her hand slipping on the stainless steel handle as she opened it. No one looked at her as she walked back to her desk and picked up her bag. She knew she ought to be thinking about how serious this was, but she couldn't keep her mind on it. Instead she found herself wondering whether Jay's phone might be on by the time she got home. It would probably be midday by then. Whatever was she going to do for money now, though? She should have asked whether she'd be paid for the whole month.

On her way out she went into the toilets. Suddenly she felt weighed down by her tiredness. In a way she was almost glad to be sent home: at least she wouldn't have to work the rest of the day. But even the walk to the tube seemed too much.

She shouldn't do it, of course. She should leave the building now with whatever speck of dignity she had left, but all she wanted was a little rest. The tiles of the cubicle floor were cold and hard against her bones, so she pulled her coat over her to keep herself warm. Curled around the base of the toilet with her back against the door, she went to sleep.

After that she found herself a job at the photocopy shop pretty quickly, but of course the money wasn't the same. Suddenly she had to scale down her habit and it wasn't pleasant. So one lunch hour she decided to try supplementing her wages. She was sick of feeling so terrible all the time.

She pushed open the heavy glass door of Morley's, Brixton's extraordinary dinosaur of a department store, and paused by the escalator, trying to think. Surely it wouldn't be hard. Their security was absurdly slack, as befitted a shop which appeared to have got stuck in the Thirties. Once or twice, when stoned and carefree, she had stolen pointless things, a cheap necklace, a notebook with a picture of an owl on the cover, purely for the hell of it.

Now, though, she would have to be more considered.

Downstairs was kitchenware, upstairs were sewing equipment and strange, old-fashioned women's underwear. She decided she'd be better off with clothes. She began to wander through the Top Shop section, ruffling through rails of skirts, tops and dresses in what she hoped was an imitation of a casual shopper, though her jangling nerves and hunched shoulders hampered her memory of what that might be like. She found some thick-knit jumpers and decided they might raise a decent price. She stood stroking them thoughtfully, wondering if she should take them into the changing room. Then her hand touched a clunky plastic security tag. What had she been thinking of? Darren would be ashamed of her.

Her eyes came to rest on a display of tights and stockings. Now that was better: no security tags, small enough to fit in her bag and quite expensive, some of them. She flicked through the packets, checking the prices. Eight pounds, twelve, this was good. She tried to look around in a non-suspicious way. It had been so much easier when she'd had drugs to make her fearless. All she'd had today were the piss-coloured rinsings of yesterday's cottons. She felt shivery and her bones were sore.

Picking up three pairs of luxury tights, she strolled towards the stairs where she'd be out of sight. She had started to sweat unpleasantly. Then five yards in front of her she noticed a security guard in a stupid phoney uniform. It was as if he'd materialised out of nowhere. He was staring right at her. His eyes met hers.

If she'd had the energy, she'd have hated him. What had made him pick her out? As it was, all she wanted was to go home to bed, but she'd be doing no such thing; there were four hours of work still to go. Stuffing the tights back in the rack, she headed out into the cold again.

As she trudged back to work, a passing schoolboy said hello. He was walking along with some friends, eating a burger. She smiled and returned his hello, wondering where she knew him from. Then she remembered: they'd scored from him a few times in the summer. He'd been helping Steve out for a while.

For a moment she considered asking if he had anything on him, if he could maybe give her credit, but even in her desperate state she could see how unlikely this was. There was no way he'd be working when he was still wearing his uniform.

It wasn't just the money, though: everything was wrong. Even her health, which she'd never had much trouble with before. Something terrible was happening to her stomach; she didn't know why, after all this time. It hurt her constantly, especially at night, when the pain of it would often wake her, and she could hardly keep down any food. A hit would subdue the pain, but at the same time it would set her off vomiting. She vomited up food, tea, even water and when that was gone she vomited bitter green bile. Thin to start with, she got thinner and thinner, until clothes which were previously tight hung off her like an anorexic's. Her hip bones jutted out in blunt, flat triangles next to her swollen, sore, constipated belly.

For three days she was beset by violent diarrhoea. One moment she was lying in bed holding an even sorer stomach than usual, the next she had liquid shit running into her crotch. She walked around gingerly with a wad of toilet paper stuffed into her knickers in imitation of an adult nappy and slept with the same at night.

She had become thirsty for her own blood. She pursued it endlessly, desperately probing for its underground rivers beneath the scarred and barren surface.

Each payday she would celebrate with an extra quarter for herself, a night of abundance amid this relentless, hungry getting-by.

And one evening she messed up. Even as she put it in the

spoon she knew it was too much. She took a little speck out again with the corner of the swab wrapper and as for what was left, she thought, fuck it. She had a strong constitution and besides, it had been a rotten week. She needed a good hit.

Getting the shot in took a while, as ever, and left a bleeding trail of damage around various parts of her body. She went into the bathroom to rinse out the needle, then as the heat of the hit began to come on, she sat down on the bath mat to enjoy it.

She never felt it.

All she knew was that it was sometime later. For some reason she was lying on the bathroom floor. Woozily she pushed herself upright and tried to get to her feet. There was a roaring in her ears like some huge waterfall. She could hardly hear. She was frightened she'd gone deaf. And there was a strange taste in her mouth. It was hard to stand up; she felt all wrong. She staggered along a tunnel to her bed, everything outside that narrow focus dark and confused. As soon as she lay down she felt sick, but she couldn't move from the bed. She vomited onto the carpet, then passed out again.

The next day she felt sick again as soon as she woke up. Stepping in a slimy pool of vomit, she hurried to the toilet. She made herself tea, then slumped down on the sofa. Something wasn't right. Everything sounded muffled and woolly. Her head and her side felt bruised. Running her tongue around her mouth, the inside of her lips was raw. Then pieces of the night before came back to her. She began to put them together. The strange taste in her mouth, it must have been blood. That's why her mouth was sore. She must have fallen onto the floor and bitten her lip. The dreadful truth of it put a cold, dark weight in her stomach. An overdose, after all this time.

It was so strange that that was how it happened. The nothingness of it shocked her. Or rather, she was shocked by the nature of that nothingness. She had spent so long chasing oblivion, taking it in little doses, and all the while she had imagined it was something wonderful, something metaphysical and spectacular, velvety and huge and ancient. But it wasn't something at all, it was just nothing. No bliss, no relief, just a hissing, dead TV screen, only less.

Later when she was feeling stronger she went out for cigarettes and milk. Outside the newsagent's she ran into her old friend Patrick. True, she hadn't seen much of him lately, but they'd been quite close at one time, drinking buddies of a Friday night.

'Hi, how are you?' she asked. God, it was nice to see a familiar face.

'Yeah, I'm OK, pretty busy and all. How are you?'

'OK, yeah.' But then she remembered she wasn't OK at all. She had nearly died, alone on her bathroom floor. It would have been like one of those stories local papers always carry, where pensioners die and their bodies aren't found for weeks. She didn't have much in the way of human needs these days: she managed to meet most of them with heroin, but all at once the loneliness gripped her hard around the ribs. She desperately wanted to tell someone what had happened.

'Well, actually,' she was mumbling a little, 'I'm not that great. I OD'd last night. I mean, I came round on my own, I didn't go to hospital or anything . . . '

The look on his face brought her up short. She'd never seen anyone so appalled.

'I'm sorry,' he stuttered. 'I mean, I wish I could talk to you, but I'm actually in a rush.' He was backing away from her. 'But if you want to call me or whatever . . . '

The words were lost as he hurried away.

CHAPTER 14

It was difficult even getting into the record shop on time. She would put on something nice, maybe a skirt or jeans and then she'd feel dreadful. The way the skirt exposed the curve of her waist or the jeans hugged her arse, it made her hate herself. She'd put on make-up, a bit of eyeliner, mascara, lipstick, nothing flashy, just trying to look decent. Then she'd panic and have to wash it all off again. Asking people to look at her like that, inviting men to notice her, to touch her. She knew the clock was ticking on and she should be out of the door, but she was trapped. Piles of clothes grew on the floor as she put on one thing, then another, then pulled them off in horror. Some days she would end up walking down the road in a skirt and a snug top and despise herself for the rest of the day, terrified of what might happen. But mostly she wore baggy trousers, shapeless sweatshirts, as many layers as possible, anything to cover up this dangerous body and its reckless, noisy presence.

Her veins were shouting at her, crying out for the needle. She was sure she was going to die.

She told the counsellor that it was too much, she was all

used up, she couldn't cope with any more.

The counsellor nodded. 'I know. It's very hard for you now.'

That was all. There was no extra help for her that she'd been keeping in reserve.

'Is it like this for everyone?'

'Everyone's different, but yes, it's a hard thing to face up to. And coupled with recovery, the process of your body healing, this period when your emotions are really coming back to you . . .'

'So other people go through the same thing?'

'It's . . . it's not uncommon.' The counsellor sighed. 'The kind of despair which results in a life-threatening addiction, it doesn't come from nowhere. As counsellors we have to consider that some people's lives are really that bleak; that poverty has left them with that little. Then there's also the impact of trauma. You find that a lot of addicts have suffered some kind of fairly serious abuse, and when you stop suppressing it with drugs, it tends to come back to you. And sexual abuse is one of the ones we come across the most.'

How useless Esther was, how pathetic. It was as common as rain and she alone couldn't deal with it. She tried to throw it in casually: 'And other people manage to cope.'

'Some do, some don't.'

'I don't know if I definitely want to go,' Esther said one time when her dad was due to come and pick her and Dominic up for their weekly visit.

'Oh Esther, you know your dad's all on his own now. He'd be so upset if he didn't see you.'

And she knew her mum was right. Her mum couldn't look after him anymore. She was the eldest and it was down to her to be nice to him now that he didn't have anyone else. She didn't know why she'd even said anything so mean.

The doorbell rang and he didn't come in; he never did. He

just stood there waiting, looking cold on the doorstep, while she and Dominic put their coats on.

There was a funny smell to the flat, slightly musty and closed up, but something else too, a suggestion of chemicals or glue. When he'd first moved in he'd complained that the carpet smelt, that the landlady must have got it cheap after some factory spillage. The smell had never quite gone. Whenever they opened the front door, it made her stomach sink.

Sometimes they went out places, like the pictures or the park or to the Wimpy for chips and a milkshake, but sometimes, like today, they just stayed in watching TV. There were a lot of Westerns on in the afternoons, but this time it was James Bond. Sexy women kept trying to trick him, but he was always too clever for them.

Then they were all in the kitchen, fetching squash and biscuits. Her dad stopped and hugged her, holding her for a long time as they stood still in the middle of the room. The rough wool of his jumper pressed against her face. He released her a little and bent his face down towards her. Dominic wasn't there, he'd disappeared somewhere. The rims of her dad's eyes were pink. They looked naked within their pale lashes, like some underground creature exposed to the light, helpless but at the same time frightening and wrong. This time he didn't kiss her on the lips. He lowered his head further and kissed the base of her neck, where it curves into the collar bone. His mouth was moist.

But she wasn't there. She had gone. She knew it looked like her body and she could still see the clock over his shoulder with its red plastic frame, but Esther herself had disappeared. She was frozen, in suspension. For this moment of time she didn't exist. She had no feelings at all.

Afterwards when they got home her mum asked her if she'd had a nice time.

She said yes.

And it was all over until the next week, when he'd put the key in the door and that smell would be in her nostrils, opening up a hole deep inside her, the awful, secret truth of what a revolting person she was.

Now she was really in a mess. She could hardly function. From some numb, still place inside she watched herself, amazed at how she kept on going. It seemed bizarre that she was still cooking meals and eating them, that she still opened the curtains in the morning, that she washed her clothes and went to work. There was something dreadful about it, like the actions of an animal or an insect, driven on by blunt instinct when all sense says it should give up, like the mother bird who sees all her offspring picked off by the same cat, but can't help leading each chirping baby out onto the branch.

The world was thick and muddy around her. It was hard to keep pushing through it. The food in her mouth was heavy and dry. At night sometimes her heart would seize up and stop still in her chest. She would listen to the stillness and think, thank God. But then with a judder it would start beating again.

Every movement that she made, every word she spoke appalled her. The way she washed the dishes was the way an abused person washed them. So was the way she sat down on the tube. The sight of her skin was unbearable: a bare arm, an ankle were too vulnerable. They shouted sex. They were going to make men come near her, slip an arm around her, slide their hands over her. She was giving off the smell of it and there was nothing she could do.

She couldn't stand the feel of her knickers in her crotch. The dampness of her cunt made her want to put a rope around her neck.

She didn't know how she was still alive, or why.

In the bath she wanted to slide down until her head was

underwater and then stay there. By the door to the flat, as she put down her shopping and took out her keys, she wanted to smash her head against the bricks. It was hard to wait as she crossed the road. She wanted to step out into the moving traffic. She wanted to eat pills or poison, a plastic jar, a dark blue bottle. She wanted to step into the lift of some high block, climb onto the balcony wall and jump. How fast the concrete would rush towards her; she wondered if she'd feel it. She wanted to take the breadknife to her throat, a razor to her wrists. She wanted it to hurt and then be over.

She was thankful for her job; it kept her body busy for whole chunks of time while her mind spun round and round in this tornado.

On her days off and in the evenings she would put a CD on and get into bed with a T-shirt over her head. She was listening to Elliott Smith obsessively, the same records over and over, getting up and pressing 'play' when they finished. On 'Angeles' a ringing sound, like a finger on the rim of a wineglass, was the sound of pain itself, the way you hear it in your head. She wanted heroin so much, the tidy violence of the needle, the relief, the blankness. She wasn't sure she'd ever wanted it more. But if she just stayed in bed she wouldn't be able to score. She gritted her teeth and lay there, waiting for something to happen, one way or the other.

Maybe he'd wanted to claim her for himself, to feel warm and loved, to have someone who belonged to him alone, divided from her mother by this secret. How could she know, when she still wasn't sure he'd done it?

Sometimes she almost believed it was true, this story she was telling, but it was hard when she'd spent so long convinced that none of it had touched her. It was strange how easy it had been: after the first time, she'd simply stepped backwards out of her body whenever he'd come near her. As much as she'd thought anything, which she hadn't, she'd believed that she'd been out of his reach. But the first time, she had to admit, he had got her. She could still remember her confusion when he'd said it, her surprise, her shock at what a disgusting thing she'd done. She'd thought it had just been a daughterly kiss goodbye, but then he'd told her, 'You're a better kisser than your mother.'

Could it be true, that that was his reason? A piece of spite against her mother, of revenge on her for leaving him? It whited out her reason, this question of how he could have done it, but maybe he'd simply thought nothing. Just the whine of self-pity in his ears, and the birthright in the cells of his skin and bones and fibres, the right of conquest. Maybe just the whisper that he deserved it and besides, no one would notice. With those tokens of sex he'd established that Esther was his. He didn't even need to fuck her, because the outcome if he'd tried was already decided. Her mother had refused his control, but in this teenage girl he found a piece of womanhood he could subdue.

Yet how could it be true? What was missing in him, that all he saw was the daughter of the woman who had left him? How had he been so removed from the child he was meant to care for, that his revenge was all that mattered? How had he forgotten that she was his daughter too?

The spirals of it made her dizzy, standing on so much unreality. Everything solid had gone. If she'd been talking about strangers, it might have made some sense, but she was talking about her dad.

As she lay in bed with the music filling her head, she wondered what she was waiting for. In her disconnected way, she found it strange. What was it that stopped her taking that leap or opening up that vein? It didn't seem to be anything as definite as hope. Maybe animal instinct was all it was, or some buried seam of doubt that things could really stay the same.

CHAPTER 15

And gradually, as the months went by, it did get better. Some days were good and some were bad, but the panic and horror were no longer constant. The awful fact was still a fact, but it began to shrink in size so that it no longer filled her whole field of vision. Sometimes the concept of life no longer seemed so strange to her and these good days were like premonitions, glimpses of a future which was surely coming her way. Where once she would have counted it no favour for her life to have been saved, sometimes now she forgot for hours or even days why she'd been so obsessed with dying. At these moments what had once been the whole shape of the world seemed like a dream or another life. Maybe she was going to stay alive.

As time drew on towards a year since she'd kicked, she could feel how her body had recovered. She craved fruit and vegetables, instead of cakes and chocolate like she used to. She had a healthy person's energy and it didn't always feel like a joke at her expense. She began to think about giving up smoking. She never would have guessed it would all take so long. It was funny to think how when she'd kicked she'd imagined she'd be better in a couple of months. Who'd have thought a little drug-taking could turn out so serious?

Once a week, on her day off, she went swimming. She began to get muscles in her arms. She bought houseplants and fed and watered them so that they stayed alive. She went on a daytrip to the country with Lucia and Gareth. As they walked along muddy tracks with the cold wind in their faces and the grey, English sky above them, she felt fabulously proud of herself. It was like being a newborn person in the world. Things that other people found ordinary, like paying their bills before the threats arrived or filling their cupboards with food, were impressive and exciting to her. She was no longer killing herself day in, day out, with dirty powder bought in a wrap of tangled clingfilm spat out of a dealer's mouth. She was no longer compulsive, enchained, degraded. Her shame had turned to pride, in the same measure. She had done something amazing. She'd never known she had so much strength. It had been really, bloody hard, but she'd got out.

She started calling her relatives from time to time. She could chat to old women at bus stops or customers in the shop without wishing that they'd leave her alone. Sometimes she got a weird feeling that she was part of humanity and that instead of fighting against it, she could fight with it; that the majority of people deserved something better than this.

Sometimes she felt happy for no reason.

It had seemed so mysterious and exciting, this addiction. It was almost a comedown to find it was so prosaic, just one reaction of many to trauma and abuse. A simple, terrible thing, with a simple, terrible cause. Like the oblivion which had called her for so long, she was surprised to find it so flat and sad. Whether people were fascinated by addiction or despised it, they always seemed to think it was something less straightforward. But really she was relieved. Now that she knew what it was, it wasn't so powerful. It gave her a chance.

As Christmas drew near, London put on its festive glitter. The council put up the Christmas lights in Brixton, a battered collection of plastic Santa Clauses and reindeer and snowflakes made of coloured lightbulbs, the same assortment it had been wheeling out for years, strapped onto the same lampposts on the highstreet. The record shop grew busier as people came in to do their Christmas shopping, buying a worse selection of music than ever. Esther still liked the season no more than before; she hadn't become that much of a drone. She tried to ignore it but there was little escape. Fringed gold banners hung in every shop window behind the spray-on fake snow and every doorway blared out compilations of appalling Christmas songs.

One of her co-workers, Becky, invited all the shop's staff to her Christmas party.

'Thanks, that'd be great,' said Esther, with no intention of going. The prospect of a party alarmed her. She hadn't been out much this past year: she was scared of drinking and she felt self-conscious with her mineral water while everyone else ordered spirits and beer.

But in the end Justin persuaded her to go. He'd invited the glamorous Saffy from his now hibernating band and he wanted Esther there to support him. It had taken him two years to ask Saffy anywhere, possibly that long even to speak to her. Reluctantly Esther consented.

She called round to collect him on a cold, rainy Saturday night. His pink-haired housemate let her in and she climbed the stairs to his room.

'Hold on!' he called from behind the closed door.

'It's Esther.'

'Won't be a sec.'

She sighed and waited. She didn't know why he bothered. It wasn't as if there was any mystery about what he was doing. When he opened the door a bitter smell of burning hung in the air. A possibility tugged at her insides. Maybe it would be a good idea, just this once, to see her through the party. She tried to freeze the train of thought before it could gather pace.

'I've just got to get changed,' he said. 'D'you think this is OK?' He held up a T-shirt with a picture of Sonic Youth on the front.

'Yeah, sure.'

He looked bashful. 'Don't you think Saffy looks a bit like her?' He pointed at the image of Kim Gordon.

'No, not really.'

Down by the tube the pavements were packed with dressed up people and a dangerous convergence of umbrellas. Buses splashed towards the bus stops. She and Justin bought travelcards from the junkies by the station's entrance. With a sudden marketplace spirit, Esther tried to haggle.

'Two quid? Why, how much did you pay for it?'

He looked outraged. 'Nothing, of course, but this is my job!'

Charmed, she handed him the money. Clearly she'd been trying to undercut a union rate.

They were headed for Finsbury Park. Justin's eyelids drooped shut beside her. Now that it was safe she allowed herself a moment of longing. How she wished she was as stoned as him.

The train was full of young men and women in their best clothes, finishing their make-up, swigging from cans, eyeing each other up, talking loudly across the carriage. What would it be like, she wondered, to flirt with someone, to try to pick them up? It felt as if she'd been indoors forever, playing snakes and ladders with sanity. Out here she was dazzled by the display of hormones. She couldn't remember what it was like to want someone.

The thud of the music made the house easy enough to find. A man she didn't know opened the door.

'Friends of Becky's,' she shouted over the party noise. He nodded vaguely and stood back to let them in. Esther had two bottles of Budvar in a plastic bag; Justin had nothing. They went from room to room, Esther hanging around idly by the door as Justin searched each one for his beloved Saffy.

'She's not here. Do you think she's already left? We were a bit late, weren't we?'

'Dunno, I doubt it. She'll probably be here soon.' They were in the kitchen now. Esther found a bottle opener and took the lid off her beer. She spotted the hostess, Becky, in a corner. She was wearing a Sixties skirt suit, as she usually did, with thick sweeps of eyeliner below her straight-cut fringe. Esther nodded to her and mouthed hello. She took a swig of beer, then lit a cigarette. It was hard to know what to do; Justin wasn't bubbling with chat, but then nor was she. She poked idly at the magnets on the fridge. There was a whole colony of words on the freezer compartment. In a wonky line someone had written 'Your lemon bagel sleeps head first tonight.'

' 'Scuse me.' Someone beside her was trying to get into the fridge.

She stood aside to give him room to rummage. He had a nice haircut, unkempt but pleasing. He smiled at her as he shut the door, three bottles in his hand, and she smiled back. It was like a momentary hallucination, a vision of the life which might have been.

Justin had disappeared; she supposed he'd gone to look for Saffy again. She stubbed out her cigarette, then lit another. She was starting to feel weird. The beer had gone straight to her head, though she hadn't even finished the bottle. It was ridiculous. What sort of freak was she, unable even to manage a bottle of beer? But it was no use. The loose-jointed feeling in her head was too disturbing. She put the bottle down and poured herself a cup of orange juice instead.

Around her in the kitchen other people were drinking, chatting, smoking. Would she be like this forever, she wondered, a social outcast, defined by her past?

The shop's manager, Nick, came over and said hello.

'How're you doing?' he asked.

'OK, yeah. And you?'

'Yeah, I'm fine.' He nodded. There was a pause. Esther looked distractedly at his thinning, fair hair and soft features and tried to think of something to say. Did the orange juice in her hand make it obvious she was an ex-junkie? Was she going to be sacked now her secret was out?

'Done your Christmas shopping yet?' he managed at last.

Something imploring in his tone suddenly made sense to her. 'Some of it. Terry Pratchett book for my brother, scarf for my Grandma, you know how it is.' It struck her as extraordinary that he'd mistaken her for a normal human being who might go home with someone from a party, but she was relieved that he didn't know how wrong he was.

Nick struggled through a little more conversation, then wandered away. Esther joined a queue of people waiting for the toilet. There was some unmistakable huffing and foot-shuffling going on.

'What are you doing in there?' the bloke at the front of the queue shouted through the door.

There was no reply.

'Maybe they've passed out,' someone else suggested hopefully. 'We might have to kick the door in.'

At last the lock slid back and out came Justin. He stumbled past Esther without even seeing her. He was in another world. Esther was shocked. It was only a couple of hours since his last hit. She hadn't realised he was using so much. Then she was jealous.

Once again she tried to shut herself off from the thought process that was setting out around the pathways of her brain.

Esther wandered into the living room to see if she'd be any happier there. She chatted with another of her workmates, Colin.

'Hey, Colin.' The man with the nice haircut who'd been rummaging in the fridge earlier appeared at his side. 'How's it going?' The cigarette in his hand was down to the filter, with a long stalk of ash. As he looked around him for an ashtray the cylinder of ash dived straight into Esther's plastic cup.

'Oh shit. I'm sorry. I'll go and get you another one.' He grinned and Esther had a feeling she hadn't had for a long time. There seemed to be too many teeth in his mouth and they were all crooked. Somehow it made her look at his mouth for too long. 'What were you drinking?'

'Orange juice.'

'Just orange juice?'

'I'm on antibiotics.'

'At Christmas? Unlucky.' He took her cup and disappeared.

Ten minutes later she'd forgotten him when he nudged her elbow and handed her another cup of juice.

'Sorry it took so long. Some bloke was sick on my trainers.'

'He wasn't wearing a Sonic Youth T-shirt, was he?'

'Dunno. Might've been. What's your name anyway?'

She smiled. 'Esther.'

He shook her hand. 'I'm Danny.' He had dark eyes, not as pretty as Irfan's, but still appealing. His cheeks were lean and scarred by acne. He smiled again and out came all those teeth. Could I really do this, she wondered?

They sat down on a sofa together. Esther couldn't believe it: it was like balancing along a high wall, but somehow she was doing it. The heat of his body beside her was shocking. It was so long since she'd been close to another human being.

It turned out he was a librarian.

'You don't look like a librarian,' Esther observed.

'No, everyone says that. But I really like it, the index system, keeping everything in order, the network of other libraries.'

Esther smiled approvingly. 'Yes, I know what you mean.'

'And I'm planning to make a film as well. It's going to be about this bloke – well, he works in a library, actually – who finds out about a plan to store drugs in the reference section. But in fact it turns out it's all a plot by the government... Anyway, I've got it all worked out. It's just raising the money that's the hard part.'

'Why, how much have you got so far?'

'Well, nothing as yet. But like I said, that is the hard part.'

She kept forgetting that she was too crazy to sleep with him. A secret argument was replaying over and over in her head. She'd tell herself that she should stop this now, it was bound to end in trouble, but then he'd say something which defused all her doubts and she'd find herself chatting away as if she wasn't a mad person at all. Then she'd remember and it would all begin again.

The night drew on until it was clearly late, but it seemed they were both afraid to draw attention to the fact.

Esther steeled herself. It was getting ridiculous. 'Well, I guess I should be going.' She patted her thighs in the manner of someone about to get up.

'Oh right. Well, it was really nice talking to you. I mean, maybe I could take your number...' He shrugged diffidently.

'Uh huh, sure.' Did she sound disappointed? There was a pause.

'That is,' he took a deep breath, 'unless you fancy coming back with me?'

A piece of sunshine lit up inside her. 'Yes, I'd like to.'

He grinned with another flash of wonky teeth. They both stood up.

'I've just got to look for my cousin, check how he's getting home.'

She went from room to room, but found no sign of Justin. Then in a corner behind a door she spotted him. All the furniture had been moved out of this room and a few lively souls were still dancing to the pounding music. He was sound asleep.

'Justin, Justin!' It was hard to make herself heard. She reached down and shook his shoulder.

He opened his eyes. 'Uh, what?'

'I'm going now,' she shouted.

'Oh shit, did I miss it all?'

She shrugged. 'I suppose so.'

He didn't look particularly disappointed. 'Saffy didn't come, did she?'

'No.'

'Oh well.' He smiled ruefully and pushed himself to his feet.

She and Danny called a minicab and Justin went to catch the nightbus. Whereas they'd found no shortage of conversation amid the noise of the party, now in the taxi they both fell silent. Arriving among the kebab shops and litter of Kentish Town, they hurried through the rain to his front door. He went into the living room ahead of her, picking up stray socks and sweatshirts along the way.

'It's normally really tidy...'

Esther followed him, still tongue-tied, and sat down on a sofa covered with a blue patterned bedspread. The springs sagged comfortably beneath her.

'Tea?' he offered.

She nodded. While he was in the kitchen she looked around. There was a poster of Clint Eastwood on the wall in a dusty black cowboy outfit. Beneath it on the mantelpiece were a couple of dying cacti. On the coffee table beside her she noticed a piece of notepaper with the word 'PLAN' written at the top. It was underlined three times. The rest was blank.

Danny brought in two steaming mugs of tea and put them on the table. He sat down beside her. The room was quiet. From the street outside came the sound of two people exchanging shouts of abuse. She couldn't tell whether they were fighting or joking.

'Shall I put some music on?' Danny asked.

'OK, sure.' She glanced at him, then didn't know how to look away. For a moment neither of them moved. She was going to do it, that thing she'd been thinking about since she'd first looked at his mouth.

As they kissed, strange feelings surged up inside her. She didn't know what they were. It was all a mess. It was too much. Her feelings were drowning her. Her eyes stung with tears, then overflowed; she couldn't stop them. She kept on kissing him, partly because she wanted to and partly because when they stopped he'd see that she was crying. The heat of his mouth was wonderful and the tears flooded down her face.

They drew apart and she tried to turn her face away.

He looked shocked. 'What's wrong?'

'Nothing. I'm sorry...' What a wretched creature she was. The first good thing in ages and she'd ruined it. It was obvious: she was incapable of being close to anyone without drugs to protect her. She jumped up and grabbed her coat. She'd have to get away now before it got worse.

'What's the matter?' He stood up too. 'Did I do something wrong? I didn't mean to...'

'I'm sorry.' She was struggling to get her coat on. She had to get out of the door before she started crying any more.

'Don't go.'

'I'm really sorry.' It was stupid to keep repeating it, but she couldn't think what else to say. If she tried to explain he'd know how crazy she was. She pulled the door open and ran down the stairs; she didn't look back. In the anonymity of the dark wet night she could breathe again.

The taxi driver took her into Brixton by a back route. On a sudden impulse she asked him to stop.

'I'll get out here.' Had that been a light she'd seen in Justin's window?

She didn't want to wake the whole house, so she tried throwing stones up at the window. There was definitely a glimmer of light there, though of course that didn't mean he was awake. She had trouble getting the stones to reach that high. At last the curtain moved and Justin's face peeked out. She waved vigorously.

As he opened the door he looked deeply confused. 'I thought you went off with that bloke?'

'Yeah, I just . . . it just turned out stupid.'

'Right, sure.' He nodded quickly, clearly concerned that she might tell him more. 'D'you want to come up?'

In his room the TV was on. Lying on the floor among the clutter were a needle and a spoon.

'I was just watching this thing about Ibiza. It looks really crap.'

Justin got under his duvet and Esther slouched against the edge of the mattress. She felt drained and empty. The footage on TV was of the inside of a nightclub. Young women in bikini tops were waving their hands in the air as the camera zoomed in towards their navels. The programme finished and was followed by a show about motor racing. As the cars wound round and round the track she wondered if it might be the most boring pursuit on earth.

'I'd better go,' she said when it ended.

Justin opened his eyes. 'Oh, sure.' He wasn't looking well,

she noticed. He was getting that funny waxy pale colour like a proper junkie. 'Crash here if you want.' He was falling asleep as he said it.

She hesitated. Generally she liked to be in her own place, but it suddenly struck her why she'd come here: she was lonely. She needed another person near her, to stand between her and the vast space that was out there. Not to ask her questions or to stir up those awful things called needs and desires. Just someone to know if she was dead or alive.

She stripped down to her vest and pants and got under the duvet beside him. Lying with her back to him, she willed sleep to come and stop her thinking. Justin put one arm loosely over her and together they slipped into unconsciousness.

CHAPTER 16

'Jesus Christ, Darren. What happened?' His right arm was in a sling and pieces of surgical gauze were taped to his cheek and forehead.

'I know. Look.' He lifted his sweatshirt to reveal more bandages. 'I set my bed on fire. With a ciggy.' He looked with evident mixed feelings at the cigarette currently in his hand.

Esther followed him into the flat, then gasped again. Thick swirls of smoke darkened the wall where his bed had been and the entire ceiling was black.

'Dermot lent me a lilo, though.' He pointed with his left hand.

'Fuck's sake! What were you doing? You could've died.'

'I know, I know.' The idea of having almost killed himself was clearly embarrassing. 'It was just one of those things. What can you do? They told me in casualty there've been ODs all over London. They put warnings about it in the paper, strong batch going round and all that, but I don't generally read the paper.'

Esther followed him into the kitchen while he made tea. He'd been in his new place, a tiny flat in New Cross, for a couple of months now. The previous occupant had been a homesick Indian man who had painted the walls fuchsia pink, crimson, mustard and leaf green. Darren didn't have much to fill it with, just some bags and boxes, one chair and now the lilo which had replaced the bed. He was eating his meals with a teaspoon from his only plate. For a while Esther had avoided him, but now it no longer made her so nervous to see him. Besides, it wasn't as if he made the lifestyle look exciting.

They sat down to drink their tea, Darren on the lilo and Esther on the chair. Esther told him about this and that: the latest goings-on at work, a film she'd seen, a book she'd read. 'So what've you been up to?' she asked at last.

It was always the same answer. 'Dunno, really. Nothing much.'

It was strange how this last year her life had been crushed full of changes, while for Darren every day looked so similar. She took a deep breath and asked her regular question: 'So when are you going to stop? Have you got any plans?'

He gave a small shrug and looked away. 'You know how it is. There's just been all this stuff going on. Moving house, the fire...' He trailed off.

That was it; that was the balance they kept. She would ask, once in a while, so that she didn't feel she was closing her eyes to his destruction, but she wouldn't press it further. To do so would have been to forget her own recent past. Deep down Darren knew well enough the state he was in, or, at least, he must surely know sometimes, in the mornings or on Sundays or any day he couldn't scrabble together the money to score.

After a while she stood up to go.

'Actually, Esther,' Darren said quickly, 'I wanted to ask you a favour.'

'Uh huh?'

'Could I borrow a bit of money off you?'

Reluctantly she handed him the ten pound note in her purse,

then set off homewards. Waiting for the bus, she felt depressed and suddenly angry. Why couldn't he sort himself out? It was bad enough leading such a nothing of a life, but what about the next accident or the one after that? She resented being friends with someone who might die at any moment.

When she got home the light was flashing on her answerphone. Still thinking about Darren, she made herself some toast, then she remembered the message. As soon as she heard her dad's voice she almost stopped listening. She hated hearing from him. She hated the effort of mental shutdown she had to make in order to speak to him.

But this time there was something different in his voice. 'Esther, it's your dad. I'm afraid I've got some bad news. It's about your cousin, Justin. Please can you ring me as soon as you get this.'

Much as she didn't want to, she picked up the phone.

At the funeral Justin's mother, father, sister and brother walked together towards the crematorium. They all had the same look about them: pale, drawn and numb, as if they'd been starved for a week, then hit over the head with a heavy object. Other relatives clustered around them, as if to guide them forwards.

Inside they were the first to take their places. Justin's brother put an arm around his big sister, trying to act older than his sixteen or so years. For a moment his sister pressed her face into his shoulder, then she dried her eyes with a tissue and faced forwards again.

But Esther could hardly bear it, the lowered voices and the sombre movements of the other mourners. They were smothering her. Rage was snapping around her body like loose electricity and she didn't know how long she could contain it. Her limbs felt rigid and brittle, ready to break apart at the least collision, and she stepped every step like a robot or a toy soldier come to life, a blink away from lashing out. If anyone crossed her, she'd show them. Though who she had in mind, she wasn't sure.

Instead, she had to draw herself in all the more. She got stuck sitting next to her dad, just as she'd feared, and his leg and hip kept nudging against hers. The pew was too full for her to pull away. She was struggling to hold her memory under, to be blank and new, to exist only in this moment.

The vicar told them how much everyone had liked Justin and Esther was disgusted, because what did he know? They all stood to sing the hymns, then sat down again while the vicar read slowly from the Bible, words of comfort for the living. Minute by minute Esther felt sicker, thinking how Justin would have hated it. Tears spiked her eyes and she tried to blink them back before anyone could see. She wasn't crying from sadness; it was the fury trying to get out. Damn them all for not knowing who Justin was. Damn the vicar and his stupid talk of heaven. Damn Justin for his carelessness and Irfan in whatever selfish hole he was in and the whole wide world for everything she'd been through. It was all she could do not to push her way out and leave.

Afterwards they all went to his parents' house, where there were endless trays of sandwiches, cold quiche and sausage rolls. Esther filled a paper plate and picked at the food, but it seemed she wasn't the only one who wasn't hungry. She was trying to avoid her dad, slipping out of any room he entered without passing too close. She was using a kind of radar to do it, sensing his proximity without ever looking directly at him.

In the kitchen Justin's mother and his sister, Pauline, came to talk to her. They were also balancing paper plates of food which neither of them was eating.

'I'm glad you could come,' his mum said. 'He told me you were working at the record shop with him.'

Esther nodded. 'Yeah, of course. I had to come. I mean, I'd

got to know him quite well.' A catch in her throat brought her up short.

'It's a shame not many of his friends could make it,' his mum continued. 'You know, there are old friends of his from school here, but the people he was in that group with...'

'Well, it's a difficult time, Christmas, and I'm sure they meant to...' It seemed somehow rude to mention heroin, even though the word hung heavily over them.

'It's just hard to understand...' She took a careful breath and beside her Pauline stroked her shoulder. 'It's hard to understand why he'd have wanted to do that.'

If it was a question, Esther didn't know how to answer it. 'I know,' she said lamely and they stood awkwardly for a moment, then his mum gave her a weak smile and moved away. Pauline lingered behind. Again they were quiet, though it was less awkward now.

'It's just so weird,' she said at last. 'Nearly New Year. So weird to think this year will happen without him in it.' This was more than she could say without crying. Tears darkened with mascara slid over black streaks which had already dried. She was a couple of years older than Justin, maybe twenty-three, with a family similarity that was hard to place. She had the same light blue eyes, but it was more than that; maybe it was in the way she moved and talked.

Pauline took a tissue from her pocket and dabbed at her eyes and nose. 'I heard they put warnings in the paper.'

'Oh, right. I didn't know.' Esther nodded and the lie reminded her of her guilt.

Pauline pushed herself onwards. 'Still, at least he died happy. That's what I keep telling myself.'

Esther nodded again and tried to smile. She thought of her own overdose and its sickening blankness, but she couldn't bear to puncture her bravado. 'Yes, at least there's that.'

As she left she hugged Pauline tightly. Then she got into the car for her father to drive her to the station. She hadn't been able to think of any way to refuse. As they curved along green commuter lanes she tried to fill the space with talk. Sometimes her mind would go blank and the quiet would make her panic, then she'd think of something else to say. She was trying not to look at him, to keep her eyes on the road ahead, but every so often they'd stray to his hands on the gearstick or on the steering wheel as they took the corners. There were liverspots on them now and the knuckles were slightly enlarged. If she remembered now, while she was next to him, everything would implode.

The anger that had boiled in her all day had melted like a cloud. Instead there was only fear – of the word or touch with which he'd prove again that she was nothing, a person without power, to whom he could do anything. Her only protection was this hard, thin shell which said that everything was normal, that nothing had ever happened.

Of course at other times she was angry with him, in a cerebral way, when she thought about it. She despised him, that was easy. But as for feeling it, she didn't know how. When she'd stepped backwards from her body, week after week, year after year, her feelings had got lost and now she didn't know where they were. When she thought about him or when she was with him, she still found herself stuck three feet behind herself; she couldn't click back in. She could be angry with the rest of the world and, God knows, she often was, but for him she had only fear.

When they reached the station she did what she had to do. She kissed him on the cheek, trying not to exist as she did so, then she escaped into the building and was free.

When her dad had told her about Justin, her first thought had been to turn around and head straight back to Darren's. She hadn't much idea what she should be doing, but it seemed quite likely, judging by generalised guidelines, that a recent ex-junkie like herself would have to dive straight back into drugs.

So she didn't know why she'd dialled Lucia's number instead. Maybe her fingers had some good sense which her higher faculties lacked. Whatever it was, Lucia had urged her to come up to her place. 'You can't be alone now. Please, don't even wait, just come here now.'

Her boyfriend, Gareth, had opened the door to her. 'God, Esther, that's so awful.' She'd stumbled after him into the kitchen.

Lucia hugged her. 'Sit down, my dear. I'll make you some tea. We'll have dinner in a moment. You'll have to eat with us. Then you can stay on the sofa tonight. You can stay as long as you want.'

Esther was looking out at reality from somewhere else, observing its freaky normality. She had pretty much forgotten how to speak.

Lucia served up pasta with smooth, sweet, red pepper sauce. Esther had a couple of mouthfuls, but all that chewing and swallowing was too ridiculous. Afterwards, while Gareth washed up, she and Lucia sat in the living room smoking. She suspected that cigarettes were the one thing keeping her alive.

'You know what, Lu,' she said after a while, 'I think they might have made a mistake.'

Lucia looked at her.

'I don't think it can have been him they found. I mean, he's only been using less than a year. It can't happen that quickly. It must have been a friend of his.'

Lucia shook her head slowly. 'I think they'd know,' she said gently, then sighed. 'And isn't that one of the worst things with smack, that the people who are new with it have the most danger to overdose?'

Esther didn't reply. It seemed disloyal to Justin to admit he might really be dead. When her dad had first told her, she'd cried from the shock and now tears began to run down her cheeks again.

'I should have stopped him,' she whispered.

'Do you think you could have?'

She shook her head. 'No.' Then the ease with which she said this disgusted her. A sob got stuck in her throat as she tried to choke it down. It was vile to be crying about herself, about how guilty she felt, when she was here and Justin wasn't.

She had to talk quietly to keep her voice steady: 'I remember the day I realised it, that I couldn't do anything to stop him. I just thought, oh well, I'll try to help him when he wants to stop. But I'd forgotten he might not get that far. I was just making it better for myself, wasn't I?'

'But it was true.'

'I should have tried harder.'

Lucia shook her head slowly.

Another rush of tears spilled out of Esther's eyes and she mopped at them with a tissue. Her head was still spinning and she knew it would be some time until she would feel right again. From the kitchen came the sound of clinking plates and dance music on the radio. Neither of them spoke for a while.

At last Lucia broke the silence. 'It makes me think about my brother, you know. I'm the type of person who tries to make some changes in the world, to fight for myself and for other people, and I know it's good, what I do. But still, it doesn't help him, the one I want to help.'

'No,' Esther sighed. 'But it would be terrible to stop.'

'I suppose so.'

In the kitchen, cupboard doors were opened and closed and Esther caught the smell of coffee. For a few moments longer they sat quietly together.